A BANTAM PATHFINDER EDITION

Frank Manning

SHANE

"He was tall and terrible there in the road, looming up gigantic in the half-light. He was the man I saw the first day, a stranger, dark and foreboding, forging his lone way out of an unknown past in the utter loneliness of his own immovable and instinctive defiance. He was the symbol of all the dim, formless imaginings of danger and terror ... The impact of the menace that marked him was like a physical blow."

JACK SCHAEFER'S MEMORABLE NOVEL—
A MAGNIFICENT AND ENDURING STORY ABOUT
AMERICA'S OLD WEST.

D0926293

SHANE

BY JACK SCHAEFER

BANTAM BOOKS

BANTAM PATHFINDER EDITIONS

NEW YORK / TORONTO / LONDON

RLI: VLM 5 / IL 7.12

SHANE

*A Bantam Book / published by arrangement with
Houghton Mifflin Company*

PRINTING HISTORY

Houghton Mifflin edition published October 1949
2nd printing .... December 1949
3rd printing .... April 1953
Houghton Mifflin Juvenile edition published January 1954

2nd printing .... October 1955	5th printing .. September 1961
3rd printing .... June 1957	6th printing ...... June 1963
4th printing .... January 1960	7th printing .... July 1964
8th printing .... January 1966	

Houghton Mifflin Educational edition published July 1963

2nd printing .. November 1964	3rd printing .... July 1965
4th printing ..... October 1965	

Bantam edition published November 1950

2nd printing .... June 1953	3rd printing .... July 1953
4th printing ...... August 1953	

New Bantam edition published February 1955

2nd printing ... February 1955	11th printing .... June 1958
3rd printing ..... March 1955	12th printing .. December 1958
4th printing ...... May 1955	13th printing .... March 1959
5th printing .... August 1955	14th printing .. September 1960
6th printing .... October 1955	15th printing .. November 1960
7th printing .. December 1955	16th printing .... January 1961
8th printing .. February 1956	17th printing .. September 1961
9th printing .. September 1956	18th printing ...... July 1962
10th printing .... May 1957	19th printing .... October 1962

Bantam Pathfinder edition published March 1963

21st printing .... July 1963	26th printing .... May 1965
22nd printing ..... August 1963	27th printing .... October 1965
23rd printing .... October 1963	28th printing .... January 1966
24th printing .. September 1964	29th printing ...... May 1966
25th printing .. November 1964	30th printing .... August 1966
	31st printing
	32nd printing
	33rd printing

TO CARL
for my first son
my first book

1

HE RODE into our valley in the summer of '89. I was a kid then, barely topping the backboard of father's old chuck-wagon. I was on the upper rail of our small corral, soaking in the late afternoon sun, when I saw him far down the road where it swung into the valley from the open plain beyond.

In that clear Wyoming air I could see him plainly, though he was still several miles away. There seemed nothing remarkable about him, just another stray horseman riding up the road toward the cluster of frame buildings that was our town. Then I saw a pair of cowhands, loping past him, stop and stare after him with a curious intentness.

He came steadily on, straight through the town without slackening pace, until he reached the fork a half-mile below our place. One branch turned left across the river ford and on to Luke Fletcher's big spread. The other bore ahead along the right bank where we homesteaders had pegged our claims in a row up the valley. He hesitated briefly, studying the choice, and moved again steadily on our side.

As he came near, what impressed me first was his clothes. He wore dark trousers of some serge material tucked into tall boots and held at the waist by a wide belt, both of a soft black leather tooled in intricate design. A coat of the same dark material as the trousers was neatly folded and strapped to his saddle-roll. His shirt was finespun linen, rich brown in color. The handkerchief knotted loosely around his throat was black silk. His hat was not the familiar Stetson, not the familiar gray or muddy tan. It was a plain black, soft in texture, unlike any hat I had ever seen, with a creased

crown and a wide curling brim swept down in front to
shield the face.

All trace of newness was long since gone from these
things. The dust of distance was beaten into them. They
were worn and stained and several neat patches showed on
the shirt. Yet a kind of magnificence remained and with it a
hint of men and manners alien to my limited boy's ex-
perience.

Then I forgot the clothes in the impact of the man himself. He was not much above medium height, almost slight
in build. He would have looked frail alongside father's
square, solid bulk. But even I could read the endurance in
the lines of that dark figure and the quiet power in its
effortless, unthinking adjustment to every movement of
the tired horse.

He was clean-shaven and his face was lean and hard and
burned from high forehead to firm, tapering chin. His
eyes seemed hooded in the shadow of the hat's brim. He
came closer, and I could see that this was because the brows
were drawn in a frown of fixed and habitual alertness.
Beneath them the eyes were endlessly searching from side
to side and forward, checking off every item in view, missing nothing. As I noticed this, a sudden chill, I could not
have told why, struck through me there in the warm and
open sun.

He rode easily, relaxed in the saddle, leaning his weight
lazily into the stirrups. Yet even in this easiness was a suggestion of tension. It was the easiness of a coiled spring,
of a trap set.

He drew rein not twenty feet from me. His glance hit
me, dismissed me, flicked over our place. This was not
much, if you were thinking in terms of size and scope. But
what there was was good. You could trust father for that.
The corral, big enough for about thirty head if you crowded
them in, was railed right to true sunk posts. The pasture
behind, taking in nearly half of our claim, was fenced tight.
The barn was small, but it was solid, and we were raising a
loft at one end for the alfalfa growing green in the north
forty. We had a fair-sized field in potatoes that year and

father was trying a new corn he had sent all the way to Washington for and they were showing properly in weedless rows.

Behind the house, mother's kitchen garden was a brave sight. The house itself was three rooms—two really, the big kitchen where we spent most of our time indoors and the bedroom beside it. My little lean-to room was added back of the kitchen. Father was planning, when he could get around to it, to build mother the parlor she wanted.

We had wooden floors and a nice porch across the front. The house was painted too, white with green trim, rare thing in all that region, to remind her, mother said when she made father do it, of her native New England. Even rarer, the roof was shingled. I knew what that meant. I had helped father split those shingles. Few places so spruce and well worked could be found so deep in the Territory in those days.

The stranger took it all in, sitting there easily in the saddle. I saw his eyes slow on the flowers mother had planted by the porch steps, then come to rest on our shiny new pump and the trough beside it. They shifted back to me, and again, without knowing why, I felt that sudden chill. But his voice was gentle and he spoke like a man schooled in patience.

"I'd appreciate a chance at the pump for myself and the horse."

I was trying to frame a reply and choking on it, when I realized that he was not speaking to me but past me. Father had come up behind me and was leaning against the gate to the corral.

"Use all the water you want, stranger."

Father and I watched him dismount in a single flowing tilt of his body and lead the horse over to the trough. He pumped it almost full and let the horse sink its nose in the cool water before he picked up the dipper for himself.

He took off his hat and slapped the dust out of it and hung it on a corner of the trough. With his hands he brushed the dust from his clothes. With a piece of rag pulled from his saddle-roll he carefully wiped his boots. He untied the handkerchief from around his neck and rolled his sleeves and dipped his arms in the trough, rubbing thoroughly and splashing water over his face. He shook his hands dry and used the handkerchief to remove the last drops from his face. Taking a comb from his shirt pocket, he smoothed back his long dark hair. All his movements were deft and sure, and with a quick precision he flipped down his sleeves, reknotted the handkerchief, and picked up his hat.

Then, holding it in his hand, he spun about and strode directly toward the house. He bent low and snapped the stem of one of mother's petunias and tucked this into the hatband. In another moment the hat was on his head, brim swept down in swift, unconscious gesture, and he was swinging gracefully into the saddle and starting toward the road.

I was fascinated. None of the men I knew were proud like that about their appearance. In that short time the kind of magnificence I had noticed had emerged into plainer view. It was in the very air of him. Everything about him showed the effects of long use and hard use, but showed too the strength of quality and competence. There was no chill on me now. Already I was imagining myself in hat and belt and boots like those.

He stopped the horse and looked down at us. He was refreshed and I would have sworn the tiny wrinkles around his eyes were what with him would be a smile. His eyes were not restless when he looked at you like this. They were still and steady and you knew the man's whole attention was concentrated on you even in the casual glance.

"Thank you," he said in his gentle voice and was turning into the road, back to us, before father spoke in his slow, deliberate way.

"Don't be in such a hurry, stranger."

I had to hold tight to the rail or I would have fallen backwards into the corral. At the first sound of father's voice, the man and the horse, like a single being, had wheeled to face us, the man's eyes boring at father, bright and deep in the shadow of the hat's brim. I was shivering, struck through once more. Something intangible and cold and terrifying was there in the air between us.

I stared in wonder as father and the stranger looked at each other a long moment, measuring each other in an unspoken fraternity of adult knowledge beyond my reach. Then the warm sunlight was flooding over us, for father was smiling and he was speaking with the drawling emphasis that meant he had made up his mind.

"I said don't be in such a hurry, stranger. Food will be on the table soon and you can bed down here tonight."

The stranger nodded quietly as if he too had made up his mind. "That's mighty thoughtful of you," he said and swung down and came toward us, leading his horse. Father slipped into step beside him and we all headed for the barn.

"My name's Starrett," said father. "Joe Starrett. This here," waving at me, "is Robert MacPherson Starrett. Too much name for a boy. I make it Bob."

The stranger nodded again. "Call me Shane," he said. Then to me: "Bob it is. You were watching me for quite a spell coming up the road."

It was not a question. It was a simple statement. "Yes . . ." I stammered. "Yes. I was."

"Right," he said. "I like that. A man who watches what's going on around him will make his mark."

A man who watches . . . For all his dark appearance and lean, hard look, this Shane knew what would please a boy. The glow of it held me as he took care of his horse, and I fussed around, hanging up his saddle, forking over some hay, getting in his way and my own in my eagerness. He let me slip the bridle off and the horse, bigger and more powerful than I had thought now that I was close beside it, put its head down patiently for me and stood quietly while I helped him curry away the caked dust. Only once did he stop me. That was when I reached for his saddle-roll to put it to one side. In the instant my fingers touched it, he was taking it from me and he put it on a shelf with a finality that indicated no interference.

When the three of us went up to the house, mother was waiting and four places were set at the table. "I saw you through the window," she said and came to shake our visitor's hand. She was a slender, lively woman with a fair complexion even our weather never seemed to affect and a mass of light brown hair she wore piled high to bring her, she used to say, closer to father's size.

"Marian," father said, "I'd like you to meet Mr. Shane."

"Good evening, ma'am," said our visitor. He took her hand and bowed over it. Mother stepped back and, to my surprise, dropped in a dainty curtsy. I had never seen her do that before. She was an unpredictable woman. Father and I would have painted the house three times over and in rainbow colors to please her.

"And a good evening to you, Mr. Shane. If Joe hadn't called you back, I would have done it myself. You'd never find a decent meal up the valley."

She was proud of her cooking, was mother. That was one thing she learned back home, she would often say, that was of some use out in this raw land. As long as she could still prepare a proper dinner, she would tell father when things were not going right, she knew she was still civilized and there was hope of getting ahead. Then she would tighten her lips and whisk together her special most delicious biscuits and father would watch her bustling about and eat them to the last little crumb and stand up and wipe his eyes and stretch his big frame and stomp out to his always unfinished work like daring anything to stop him now.

We sat down to supper and a good one. Mother's eyes sparkled as our visitor kept pace with father and me. Then we all leaned back and while I listened the talk ran on almost like old friends around a familiar table. But I could sense that it was following a pattern. Father was trying, with mother helping and both of them avoiding direct questions, to get hold of facts about this Shane and he was dodging at every turn. He was aware of their purpose and not in the least annoyed by it. He was mild and courteous and spoke readily enough. But always he put them off with words that gave no real information.

He must have been riding many days, for he was full of news from towns along his back trail as far as Cheyenne and even Dodge City and others beyond I had never heard of before. But he had no news about himself. His past was fenced as tightly as our pasture. All they could learn was that he was riding through, taking each day as it came, with nothing particular in mind except maybe seeing a part of the country he had not been in before.

Afterwards mother washed the dishes and I dried and the two men sat on the porch, their voices carrying through the open door. Our visitor was guiding the conversation now and in no time at all he had father talking about his own plans. That was no trick. Father was ever one to argue his ideas whenever he could find a listener. This time he was going strong.

"Yes, Shane, the boys I used to ride with don't see it yet. They will some day. The open range can't last forever. The fence lines are closing in. Running cattle in big lots is good business only for the top ranchers and it's really a poor business at that. Poor in terms of the resources going into it. Too much space for too little results. It's certain to be crowded out."

"Well, now," said Shane, "that's mighty interesting. I've been hearing the same quite a lot lately and from men with pretty clear heads. Maybe there's something to it."

"By Godfrey, there's plenty to it. Listen to me, Shane. The thing to do is pick your spot, get your land, your own land. Put in enough crops to carry you and make your money play with a small herd, not all horns and bone, but bred for meat and fenced in and fed right. I haven't been at it long, but already I've raised stock that averages three hundred pounds more than that long-legged stuff Fletcher runs on the other side of the river and it's better beef, and that's only a beginning.

"Sure, his outfit sprawls over most of this valley and it looks big. But he's got range rights on a lot more acres than he has cows and he won't even have those acres as more homesteaders move in. His way is wasteful. Too much land for what he gets out of it. He can't see that. He thinks we small fellows are nothing but damned nuisances."

"You are," said Shane mildly. "From his point of view, you are."

"Yes, I guess you're right. I'll have to admit that. Those of us here now would make it tough for him if he wanted to use the range behind us on this side of the river as he used to. Altogether we cut some pretty good slices out of it. Worse still, we block off part of the river, shut the range off from the water. He's been grumbling about that off and on ever since we've been here. He's worried that more of us will keep coming and settle on the other side too, and then he will be in a fix."

The dishes were done and I was edging to the door. Mother nailed me as she usually did and shunted me off to bed. After she had left me in my little back room and went to join the men on the porch, I tried to catch more of the words. The voices were too low. Then I must have dozed, for with a start I realized that father and mother were again in the kitchen. By now, I gathered, our visitor was out in the barn in the bunk father had built there for the hired man who had been with us for a few weeks in the spring.

"Wasn't it peculiar," I heard mother say, "how he wouldn't talk about himself?"

"Peculiar?" said father. "Well, yes. In a way."

"Everything about him is peculiar." Mother sounded as if she was stirred up and interested. "I never saw a man quite like him before."

"You wouldn't have. Not where you come from. He's a special brand we sometimes get out here in the grass country. I've come across a few. A bad one's poison. A good one's straight grain clear through."

"How can you be so sure about him? Why, he wouldn't even tell where he was raised."

"Born back east a ways would be my guess. And pretty far south. Tennessee maybe. But he's been around plenty."

"I like him." Mother's voice was serious. "He's so nice and polite and sort of gentle. Not like most men I've met out here. But there's something about him. Something underneath the gentleness . . . Something . . ." Her voice trailed away.

"Mysterious?" suggested father.

"Yes, of course. Mysterious. But more than that. Dangerous."

"He's dangerous all right." Father said it in a musing

way. Then he chuckled. "But not to us, my dear." And then he said what seemed to me a curious thing. "In fact, I don't think you ever had a safer man in your house."

2

IN THE MORNING I slept late and stumbled into the kitchen to find father and our visitor working their way through piles of mother's flapjacks. She smiled at me from over by the stove. Father slapped my rump by way of greeting. Our visitor nodded at me gravely over his heaped-up plate.

"Good morning, Bob. You'd better dig in fast or I'll do away with your share too. There's magic in your mother's cooking. Eat enough of these flannel cakes and you'll grow a bigger man than your father."

"Flannel cakes! Did you hear that, Joe?" Mother came whisking over to tousle father's hair. "You must be right. Tennessee or some such place. I never heard them called that out here."

Our visitor looked up at her. "A good guess, ma'am. Mighty close to the mark. But you had a husband to help you. My folks came out of Mississippi and settled in Arkansas. Me, though—I was fiddle-footed and left home at fifteen. Haven't had anything worth being called a real flannel cake since." He put his hands on the table edge and leaned back and the little wrinkles at the corners of his eyes were plainer and deeper. "That is, ma'am, till now."

Mother gave what in a girl I would have called a giggle. "If I'm any judge of men," she said, "that means more." And she whisked back to the stove.

That was how it was often in our house, kind of jolly

and warm with good feeling. It needed to be this morning because there was a cool grayness in the air and before I had even begun to slow on my second plate of flapjacks the wind was rushing down the valley with the rain of one of our sudden summer storms following fast.

Our visitor had finished his breakfast. He had eaten so many flapjacks that I had begun to wonder whether he really would cut into my share. Now he turned to look out the window and his lips tightened. But he pushed back from the table and started to rise. Mother's voice held him to his chair.

"You'll not be traveling in any such weather. Wait a bit and it'll clear. These rains don't last long. I've another pot of coffee on the stove."

Father was getting his pipe going. He kept his eyes carefully on the smoke drifting upward. "Marian's right. Only she doesn't go far enough. These rains are short. But they sure mess up the road. It's new. Hasn't settled much yet. Mighty soggy when wet. Won't be fit for traveling till it drains. You better stay over till tomorrow."

Our visitor stared down at his empty plate as if it was the most important object in the whole room. You could see he liked the idea. Yet he seemed somehow worried about it.

"Yes," said father. "That's the sensible dodge. That horse of yours was pretty much beat last night. If I was a horse doctor now, I'd order a day's rest right off. Damned if I don't think the same prescription would do me good too. You stick here the day and I'll follow it. I'd like to take you around, show you what I'm doing with the place."

He looked pleadingly at mother. She was surprised and good reason. Father was usually so set on working every possible minute to catch up on his plans that she would have a tussle making him ease some once a week out of respect for the Sabbath. In bad weather like this he usually would fidget and stomp about the house as if he thought it was a personal insult to him, a trick to keep him from being out and doing things. And here he was talking of a whole day's rest. She was puzzled. But she played right up.

"You'd be doing us a favor, Mr. Shane. We don't get many visitors from outside the valley. It'd be real nice to have you stay. And besides—" She crinkled her nose at him the way she did when she would be teasing father into some new scheme of hers. "And besides—I've been waiting for an excuse to try a deep-dish apple pie I've heard tell of. It would just be wasted on these other two. They eat everything in sight and don't rightly know good from poor."

He was looking up, straight at her. She shook a finger at him. "And another thing. I'm fair bubbling with questions about what the women are wearing back in civilization. You know, hats and such. You're the kind of man would notice them. You're not getting away till you've told me."

Shane sat back in his chair. A faint quizzical expression softened the lean ridges of his face. "Ma'am, I'm not positive I appreciate how you've pegged me. No one else ever wrote me down an expert on ladies' millinery." He reached out and pushed his cup across the table toward her. "You said something about more coffee. But I draw the line on more flannel cakes. I'm plumb full. I'm starting in to conserve space for that pie."

"You'd better!" Father was mighty pleased about something. "When Marian puts her mind to cooking, she makes a man forget he's got any limits to his appetite. Only don't you go giving her fancy notions of new hats so she'll be sending off to the mail-order house and throwing my money away on silly frippery. She's got a hat."

Mother did not even notice that. She knew father was just talking. She knew that whenever she wanted anything real much and said so, father would bust himself trying to get it for her. She whisked over to the table with the coffee pot, poured a fresh round, then set it down within easy reach and sat down herself.

I thought that business about hats was only a joke she made up to help father persuade our visitor to stay. But she began almost at once, pestering him to describe the ladies he had seen in Cheyenne and other towns where the new styles might be. He sat there, easy and friendly, telling her how they were wearing wide floppy-brimmed bonnets with lots of flowers in front on top and slits in the brims for scarves to come through and be tied in bows under their chins.

Talk like that seemed foolish to me to be coming from a grown man. Yet this Shane was not bothered at all. And father listened as if he thought it was all right, only not very interesting. He watched them most of the time in a good-natured quiet, trying every so often to break in with his own talk about crops and steers and giving up and trying again and giving up again with a smiling shake of his head at those two. And the rain outside was a far distance away and meaningless because the friendly feeling in our kitchen was enough to warm all our world.

Then Shane was telling about the annual stock show at Dodge City and father was interested and excited, and it was mother who said: "Look, the sun's shining."

It was, so clear and sweet you wanted to run out and breathe the brilliant freshness. Father must have felt that way because he jumped up and fairly shouted, "Come on, Shane. I'll show you what this hop-scotch climate does to my alfalfa. You can almost see the stuff growing."

Shane was only a step behind him, but I beat them to the door. Mother followed and stood watching awhile on the porch as we three started out, picking our path around the puddles and the taller clumps of grass bright with the raindrops. We covered the whole place pretty thoroughly, father talking all the time, more enthusiastic about his plans than he had been for many weeks. He really hit his stride when we were behind the barn where we could have a good view of our little herd spreading out through the pasture. Then he stopped short. He had noticed that Shane was not paying much attention. He was quiet as could be for a moment when he saw that Shane was looking at the stump.

That was the one bad spot on our place. It stuck out like an old scarred sore in the cleared space back of the barn—a big old stump, all jagged across the top, the legacy of some great tree that must have died long before we came into the valley and finally been snapped by a heavy windstorm. It was big enough, I used to think, so that if it was smooth on top you could have served supper to a good-sized family on it.

But you could not have done that because you could not have got them close around it. The huge old roots humped out in every direction, some as big about as my waist, pushing out and twisting down into the ground like they would hold there to eternity and past.

Father had been working at it off and on, gnawing at the roots with an axe, ever since he finished poling the corral. The going was slow, even for him. The wood was so hard that he could not sink the blade much more than a quarter inch at a time. I guess it had been an old burr oak. Not many of those grew that far up in the Territory, but the ones that did grew big and hard. Ironwood we called it.

Father had tried burning brushpiles against it. That old stump just jeered at fire. The scorching seemed to make the wood harder than ever. So he was fighting his way around root by root. He never thought he had much time to spare on it. The rare occasions he was real mad about something he would stomp out there and chew into another root.

He went over to the stump now and kicked the nearest root, a smart kick, the way he did every time he passed it. "Yes," he said. "That's the millstone round my neck. That's the one fool thing about this place I haven't licked yet. But I will. There's no wood ever grew can stand up to a man that's got the strength and the will to keep hammering at it."

He stared at the stump like it might be a person sprouting in front of him. "You know, Shane, I've been feuding with this thing so long I've worked up a spot of affection for it. It's tough. I can admire toughness. The right kind."

He was running on again, full of words and sort of happy to be letting them out, when he noticed again that Shane was not paying much attention, was listening to some sound in the distance. Sure enough, a horse was coming up the road.

Father and I turned with him to look toward town. In a moment we saw it as it cleared the grove of trees and tall bushes about a quarter-mile away, a high-necked sorrel drawing a light buckboard wagon. The mud was splattering from its hooves, but not bad, and it was stepping free and easy. Shane glanced sideways at father.

"Not fit for traveling," he said softly. "Starrett, you're poor shakes as a liar." Then his attention was on the wagon and he was tense and alert, studying the man upright on the swaying seat.

Father simply chuckled at Shane's remark. "That's Jake Ledyard's outfit," he said, taking the lead toward our lane. "I thought maybe he'd get up this way this week. Hope he has that cultivator I've been wanting."

Ledyard was a small, thin-featured man, a peddler or trader who came through every couple of months with things you could not get at the general store in town. He would pack in his stock on a mule-team freighter driven by an old, white-haired Negro who acted like he was afraid even to speak without permission. Ledyard would make deliveries in his buckboard, claiming a hard bargain always and picking up orders for articles to bring on the next trip. I did not like him, and not just because he said nice things about me he did not mean for father's benefit. He smiled too much and there was no real friendliness in it.

By the time we were beside the porch, he had swung the horse into our lane and was pulling it to a stop. He jumped down, calling greetings. Father went to meet him. Shane stayed by the porch, leaning against the end post.

"It's here," said Ledyard. "The beauty I told you about." He yanked away the canvas covering from the body of the wagon and the sun was bright on a shiny new seven-pronged cultivator lying on its side on the floor boards. "That's the best buy I've toted this haul."

"Hm-m-m-m," said father. "You've hit it right. That's what I've been wanting. But when you start chattering about a best buy that always means big money. What's the tariff?"

"Well, now." Ledyard was slow with his reply. "It cost

me more than I figured when we was talking last time. You might think it a bit steep. I don't. Not for a new beauty like that there. You'll make up the difference in no time with the work you'll save with that. Handles so easy even the boy here will be using it before long."

"Pin it down," said father. "I've asked you a question."

Ledyard was quick now. "Tell you what, I'll shave the price, take a loss to please a good customer. I'll let you have it for a hundred and ten."

I was startled to hear Shane's voice cutting in, quiet and even and plain. "Let you have it? I reckon he will. There was one like that in a store in Cheyenne. List price sixty dollars."

Ledyard shifted part way around. For the first time he looked closely at our visitor. The surface smile left his face. His voice held an ugly undertone. "Did anyone ask you to push in on this?"

"No," said Shane, quietly and evenly as before. "I reckon no one did." He was still leaning against the post. He did not move and he did not say anything more. Ledyard turned to father, speaking rapidly.

"Forget what he says, Starrett. I've spotted him now. Heard of him half a dozen times along the road up here. No one knows him. No one can figure him. I think I can. Just a stray wandering through, probably chased out of some town and hunting cover. I'm surprised you'd let him hang around."

"You might be surprised at a lot of things," said father, beginning to bite off his words. "Now give it to me straight on the price."

"It's what I said. A hundred and ten. Hell, I'll be out money on the deal anyway, so I'll shave it to a hundred if that'll make you feel any better." Ledyard hesitated, watching father. "Maybe he did see something in Cheyenne. But he's mixed up. Must have been one of those little makes—flimsy and barely half the size. That might match his price."

Father did not say anything. He was looking at Ledyard in a steady, unwavering way. He had not even glanced at Shane. You might have believed he had not even heard what Shane had said. But his lips were folding in to a tight line like he was thinking what was not pleasant to think. Ledyard waited and father did not say anything and the climbing anger in Ledyard broke free.

"Starrett! Are you going to stand there and let that— that tramp nobody knows about call me a liar? Are you going to take his word over mine? Look at him! Look at his clothes! He's just a cheap, tinhorn—"

Ledyard stopped, choking on whatever it was he had meant to say. He fell back a step with a sudden fear showing in his face. I knew why even as I turned my head to see Shane. That same chill I had felt the day before, intangible and terrifying, was in the air again. Shane was no longer leaning against the porch post. He was standing erect, his hands clenched at his sides, his eyes boring at Ledyard, his whole body alert and alive in the leaping instant.

You felt without knowing how that each teetering second could bring a burst of indescribable deadliness. Then the tension passed, fading in the empty silence. Shane's eyes lost their sharp focus on Ledyard and it seemed to me that reflected in them was some pain deep within him.

Father had pivoted so that he could see the two of them in the one sweep. He swung back to Ledyard alone.

"Yes, Ledyard, I'm taking his word. He's my guest. He's here at my invitation. But that's not the reason." Father straightened a little and his head went up and he gazed into the distance beyond the river. "I can figure men for myself. I'll take his word on anything he wants to say any day of God's whole year."

Father's head came down and his voice was flat and final. "Sixty is the price. Add ten for a fair profit, even though you probably got it wholesale. Another ten for hauling it here. That tallies to eighty. Take that or leave that. Whatever you do, snap to it and get off my land."

Ledyard stared down at his hands, rubbing them together as if he were cold. "Where's your money?" he said.

Father went into the house, into the bedroom where he kept our money in a little leather bag on the closet shelf. He came back with the crumpled bills. All this while Shane stood there, not moving, his face hard, his eyes following father with a strange wildness in them that I could not understand.

Ledyard helped father heave the cultivator to the ground, then jumped to the wagon seat and drove off like he was glad to get away from our place. Father and I turned from watching him into the road. We looked around for Shane and he was not in sight. Father shook his head in wonderment. "Now where do you suppose—" he was saying, when we saw Shane coming out of the barn.

He was carrying an axe, the one father used for heavy kindling. He went directly around the corner of the building. We stared after him and we were still staring when we heard it, the clear ringing sound of steel biting into wood.

I never could have explained what that sound did to me. It struck through me as no single sound had ever done before. With it ran a warmth that erased at once and forever the feeling of sudden chill terror that our visitor had evoked in me. There were sharp hidden hardnesses in him. But these were not for us. He was dangerous as mother had said. But not to us as father too had said. And he was no longer a stranger. He was a man like father in whom a boy could believe in the simple knowing that what was beyond comprehension was still clean and solid and right.

I looked up at father to try to see what he was thinking, but he was starting toward the barn with strides so long that I had to run to stay close behind him. We went around the far corner and there was Shane squared away at the biggest uncut root of that big old stump. He was swinging the axe in steady rhythm. He was chewing into that root with bites almost as deep as father could drive.

Father halted, legs wide, hands on hips. "Now lookahere," he began, "there's no call for you—"

Shane broke his rhythm just long enough to level a straight look at us. "A man has to pay his debts," he said and was again swinging the axe. He was really slicing into that root.

He seemed so desperate in his determination that I had to speak. "You don't owe us anything," I said. "Lots of times we have folks in for meals and—"

Father's hand was on my shoulder. "No, Bob. He doesn't mean meals." Father was smiling, but he was having to blink several times together and I would have sworn that his eyes were misty. He stood in silence now, not moving, watching Shane.

It was something worth seeing. When father worked on that old stump, that was worth seeing too. He could handle an axe mighty well and what impressed you was the strength and will of him making it behave and fight for him against the tough old wood. This was different. What impressed you as Shane found what he was up against and settled to it was the easy way the power in him poured smoothly into each stroke. The man and the axe seemed to be partners in the work. The blade would sink into the parallel grooves almost as if it knew itself what to do and the chips from between would come out in firm and thin little blocks.

Father watched him and I watched the two of them and time passed over us, and then the axe sliced through the last strip and the root was cut. I was sure that Shane would stop. But he stepped right around to the next root and squared away again and the blade sank in once more.

As it hit this second root, father winced like it had hit him. Then he stiffened and looked away from Shane and stared at the old stump. He began to fidget, throwing his weight from one foot to the other. In a short while more he was walking around inspecting the stump from different angles as if it was something he had never seen before. Finally he gave the nearest root a kick and hurried away. In a moment he was back with the other axe, the big double-bladed one that I could hardly heft from the ground.

He picked a root on the opposite side from Shane. He was not angry the way he usually was when he confronted one of those roots. There was a kind of serene and contented look on his face. He whirled that big axe as if it was only a kid's tool. The striking blade sank in maybe a whole half-inch. At the sound Shane straightened on his side. Their eyes met over the top of the stump and held and neither one of them said a word. Then they swung up their axes and both of them said plenty to that old stump.

3

IT WAS EXCITING at first watching them. They were hitting a fast pace, making the chips dance. I thought maybe each one would cut through a root now and stop. But Shane finished his and looked over at father working steadily away and with a grim little smile pulling at his mouth he moved on to another root. A few moments later father smashed through his with a blow that sent the axe head into the ground beneath. He wrestled with the handle to yank the head loose and he too tackled another root without even waiting to wipe off the dirt. This began to look like a long session, so I started to wander away. Just as I headed around the corner of the barn, mother came past the corner.

She was the freshest, prettiest thing I had ever seen. She had taken her hat and stripped the old ribbon from it and fixed it as Shane had told her. Some of the flowers by the house were in a small bouquet in front. She had cut slits in the brim and the sash from her best dress came around the crown and through the slits and was tied in a perky bow under her chin. She was stepping along daintily, mighty proud of herself.

She went up close to the stump. Those two choppers were so busy and intent that even if they were aware she was there they did not really notice her.

"Well," she said, "aren't you going to look at me?"

They both stopped and they both stared at her.

"Have I got it right?" she asked Shane. "Is this the way they do it?"

"Yes, ma'am," he said. "About like that. Only their brims are wider." And he swung back to his root.

"Joe Starrett," said mother, "aren't you at least going to tell me whether you like me in this hat?"

"Lookahere, Marian," said father, "you know damned well that whether you have a hat on or whether you don't have a hat on, you're the nicest thing to me that ever happened on God's green earth. Now stop bothering us. Can't you see we're busy?" And he swung back to his root.

Mother's face was a deep pink. She pulled the bow out and the hat from her head. She held it swinging from her hand by the sash ends. Her hair was mussed and she was really mad.

"Humph," she said. "This is a funny kind of resting you're doing today."

Father set the axe head on the ground and leaned on the handle. "Maybe it seems funny to you, Marian. But this is the best resting I've had for about as long as I can remember."

"Humph," said mother again. "You'll have to quit your resting for a while anyhow and do what I suppose you'll call work. Dinner's hot on the stove and waiting to be served."

She flounced around and went straight back to the house. We all tagged her in and to an uncomfortable meal. Mother always believed you should be decent and polite at mealtime, particularly with company. She was polite enough now. She was being special sweet, talking enough for the whole table of us without once saying a word about her hat lying where she had thrown it on the chair by the stove. The trouble was that she was too polite. She was trying too hard to be sweet.

As far as you could tell, though, the two men were not worried by her at all. They listened absently to her talk, chiming in when she asked them direct questions, but otherwise keeping quiet. Their minds were on that old stump and whatever it was that old stump had come to mean to them and they were in a hurry to get at it again.

After they had gone out and I had been helping mother with the dishes awhile, she began humming low under her breath and I knew she was not mad any more. She was too curious and puzzled to have room for anything else.

"What went on out there, Bob?" she asked me. "What got into those two?"

I did not rightly know. All I could do was try to tell her about Ledyard and how our visitor had called him on the cultivator. I must have used the wrong words, because, when I told her about Ledyard talking mean and the way Shane acted, she got all flushed and excited.

"What do you say, Bob? You were afraid of him? He frightened you? Your father would never let him do that."

"I wasn't frightened of him," I said, struggling to make her see the difference. "I was—well, I was just frightened. I was scared of whatever it was that might happen."

She reached out and rumpled my hair. "I think I understand," she said softly. "He's made me feel a little that way too." She went to the window and stared toward the barn. The steady rhythm of double blows, so together they sounded almost as one, was faint yet clear in the kitchen. "I hope Joe knows what he's doing," she murmured to herself. Then she turned to me. "Skip along out, Bob. I'll finish myself."

It was no fun watching them now. They had eased down to a slow, dogged pace. Father sent me once for the hone, so they could sharpen the blades, and again for a spade so he could clear the dirt away from the lowest roots, and I realized he might keep me running as long as I was handy. I slipped off by myself to see how mother's garden was doing after the rain and maybe add to the population in the box of worms I was collecting for when I would go fishing with the boys in town.

I took my time about it. I played pretty far afield. But no matter where I went, always I could hear that chopping in the distance. You could not help beginning to feel tired just to hear it, to think how they were working and staying at it.

Along the middle of the afternoon, I wandered into the barn. There was mother by the rear stall, up on a box peering through the little window above it. She hopped down as soon as she heard me and put a finger to her lips.

"I declare," she whispered. "In some ways those two aren't even as old as you are, Bob. Just the same—" She frowned at me in such a funny, confiding manner that I felt all warm inside. "Don't you dare tell them I said so. But there's something splendid in the battle they're giving that old monster." She went past me and toward the house with such a brisk air that I followed to see what she was going to do.

She whisked about the kitchen and in almost no time at all she had a pan of biscuits in the oven. While they were baking, she took her hat and carefully sewed the old ribbon into its old place. "Humph," she said, more to herself than to me. "You'd think I'd learn. This isn't Dodge City. This isn't even a whistle stop. It's Joe Starrett's farm. It's where I'm proud to be."

Out came the biscuits. She piled as many as she could on a plate, popping one of the leftovers into her mouth and giving me the rest. She picked up the plate and marched with it out behind the barn. She stepped over the cut roots and set the plate on a fairly smooth spot on top of the stump. She looked at the two men, first one and then the other. "You're a pair of fools," she said. "But there's no law against me being a fool too." Without looking at either of them again, she marched away, her head high, back toward the house.

The two of them stared after her till she was out of sight. They turned to stare at the biscuits. Father gave a deep sigh, so deep it seemed to come all the way from his heavy work shoes. There was nothing sad or sorrowful about it. There was just something in him too big to be held tight in comfort. He let his axe fall to the ground. He leaned forward and separated the biscuits into two piles beside the plate, counting them even. One was left

on the plate. He set this by itself on the stump. He took
up his axe and reached it out and let it drop gently on
the lone biscuit exactly in the middle. He rested the axe
against the stump and took the two halves of the biscuit
and put one on each pile.

He did not say a word to Shane. He pitched into one
pile and Shane did into the other, and the two of them
faced each other over the last uncut roots, munching at
those biscuits as if eating them was the most serious business they had ever done.

Father finished his pile and dabbled his fingers on the
plate for the last crumbs. He straightened and stretched
his arms high and wide. He seemed to stretch and stretch
until he was a tremendous tower of strength reaching up
into the late afternoon sun. He swooped suddenly to grab
the plate and toss it to me. Still in the same movement he
seized the axe and swung it in a great arc into the root he
was working on. Quick as he was, Shane was right with
him, and together they were talking again to that old
stump.

I took the plate in to mother. She was peeling apples
in the kitchen, humming gaily to herself. "The woodbox,
Bob," she said, and went on humming. I carried in stove-
lengths till the box would not hold any more. Then I
slipped out before she might think of more chores.

I tried to keep myself busy down by the river skipping
flat stones across the current all muddy still from the rain.
I was able to for a while. But that steady chopping had a
peculiar fascination. It was always pulling me toward the
barn. I simply could not grasp how they could stick at it
hour after hour. It made no sense to me, why they should
work so when routing out that old stump was not really so
important. I was wavering in front of the barn, when I
noticed that the chopping was different. Only one axe was
working.

I hurried around back. Shane was still swinging, cutting into the last root. Father was using the spade, was
digging under one side of the stump, bringing the dirt out
between the cut roots. As I watched, he laid the spade

aside and put his shoulder to the stump. He heaved against it. Sweat started to pour down his face. There was a little sucking sound and the stump moved ever so slightly.

That did it. Of a sudden I was so excited that I could hear my own blood pounding past my eardrums. I wanted to dash to that stump and push it and feel it move. Only I knew father would think I was in the way.

Shane finished the root and came to help him. Together they heaved against the stump. It angled up nearly a whole inch. You could begin to see an open space in the dirt where it was ripping loose. But as soon as they released the pressure, it fell back.

Again and again they heaved at it. Each time it would angle up a bit farther. Each time it would fall back. They had it up once about a foot and a half, and that was the limit. They could not get past it.

They stopped, breathing hard, mighty streaked now from the sweat rivulets down their faces. Father peered underneath as best he could. "Must be a taproot," he said. That was the one time either of them had spoken to the other, as far as I knew, the whole afternoon through. Father did not say anything more. And Shane said nothing. He just picked up his axe and looked at father and waited.

Father began to shake his head. There was some unspoken thought between them that bothered him. He looked down at his own big hands and slowly the fingers curled until they were clenched into big fists. Then his head stopped shaking and he stood taller and he drew a deep breath. He turned and backed in between two cut root ends, pressing against the stump. He pushed his feet into the ground for firm footholds. He bent his knees and slid his shoulders down the stump and wrapped his big hands around the root ends. Slowly he began to straighten. Slowly that huge old stump began to rise. Up it came, inch by inch, until the side was all the way up to the limit they had reached before.

Shane stooped to peer under. He poked his axe into the opening and I heard it strike wood. But the only way he could get in position to swing the axe into the opening was to drop on his right knee and extend his left leg and thigh into the opening and lean his weight on them. Then he could bring the axe sweeping in at a low angle close to the ground.

He flashed one quick glance at father beside and behind him, eyes closed, muscles locked in that great sustained effort, and he dropped into position with the whole terrible weight of the stump poised above nearly half of his body and sent the axe sweeping under in swift powerful strokes.

Suddenly father seemed to slip. Only he had not slipped. He had straightened even further. The stump had leaped up a few more inches. Shane jumped out and up and tossed his axe aside. He grabbed one of the root ends and helped father ease the stump down. They both were blowing like they had run a long way. But they would not stay more than a minute before they were heaving again at the stump. It came up more easily now and the dirt was tearing loose all around it.

I ran to the house fast as I could. I dashed into the kitchen and took hold of mother's hand. "Hurry!" I yelled. "You've got to come!" She did not seem to want to come at first and I pulled her. "You've got to see it! They're getting it out!" Then she was excited as I was and was running right with me.

They had the stump way up at a high angle. They were down in the hole, one on each side of it, pushing up and forward with hands flat on the under part reared before them higher than their heads. You would have thought the stump was ready to topple over clear of its ancient foundation. But there it stuck. They could not quite push it the final inches.

Mother watched them battling with it. "Joe," she called, "why don't you use some sense? Hitch up the team. Horses will have it out in no time at all."

Father braced himself to hold the stump still. He turned his head to look at her. "Horses!" he shouted. All the pent silence of the two of them that long afternoon through was being shattered in the one wonderful shout. "Horses! Great jumping Jehoshaphat! No! We started this with man-power and, by Godfrey, we'll finish it with manpower!"

He turned his head to face the stump once more and dropped it lower between his humped shoulders. Shane, opposite him, stiffened, and together they pushed in a fresh assault. The stump quivered and swayed a little—and hung fixed at its crazy high angle.

Father grunted in exasperation. You could see the strength building up in his legs and broad shoulders and big corded arms. His side of the upturned stump rocked forward and Shane's side moved back and the whole stump trembled like it would twist down and into the hole on them at a grotesque new angle.

I wanted to shout a warning. But I could not speak, for Shane had thrown his head in a quick sideways gesture to fling his hair from falling over his face and I had caught a glimpse of his eyes. They were aflame with a concen-trated cold fire. Not another separate discernible move-ment did he make. It was all of him, the whole man, puls-ing in the one incredible surge of power. You could fairly feel the fierce energy suddenly burning in him, pouring through him in the single coordinated drive. His side of the stump rocked forward even with father's and the whole mass of the stump tore loose from the last hold and toppled away to sprawl in ungainly defeat beyond them.

Father climbed slowly out of the hole. He walked to the stump and placed a hand on the rounded bole and patted it like it was an old friend and he was perhaps a little sorry for it. Shane was with him, across from him, laying a hand gently on the old hard wood. They both looked up and their eyes met and held as they had so long ago in the morning hours.

The silence should have been complete. It was not be-cause someone was shouting, a high-pitched, wordless shout. I realized that the voice was mine and I closed my mouth. The silence was clean and wholesome, and this was one of the things you could never forget whatever time might do to you in the furrowing of the years, an old stump on its side with root ends making a strange pattern against the glow of the sun sinking behind the far mountains and two men looking over it into each other's eyes.

I thought they should join the hands so close on the bole of the stump. I thought they should at least say something to each other. They stood quiet and motionless. At last father turned and came toward mother. He was so tired that the weariness showed in his walk. But there was no weariness in his voice. "Marian," he said, "I'm rested now. I don't believe any man since the world began was ever more rested."

Shane too was coming toward us. He too spoke only to mother. "Ma'am, I've learned something today. Being a farmer has more to it than I ever thought. Now I'm about ready for some of that pie."

Mother had been watching them in a wide-eyed wonder. At his last words she let out a positive wail. "Oh-h-h —you—you—men! You made me forget about it! It's probably all burned!" And she was running for the house so fast she was tripping over her skirt.

The pie was burned all right. We could smell it when we were in front of the house and the men were scrubbing themselves at the pump-trough. Mother had the door open to let the kitchen air out. The noises from inside sounded as if she might be throwing things around. Kettles were banging and dishes were clattering. When we went in, we saw why. She had the table set and was putting supper on it and she was grabbing the things from their places and putting them down on the table with solid thumps. She would not look at one of us.

We sat down and waited for her to join us. She put her back to us and stood by the low shelf near the stove staring at her big pie tin and the burned stuff in it. Finally father spoke kind of sharply. "Lookahere, Marian. Aren't you ever going to sit down?"

She whirled and glared at him. I thought maybe she had been crying. But there were no tears on her face. It was dry and pinched-looking and there was no color in it. Her voice was sharp like father's. "I was planning to have a deep-dish apple pie. Well, I will. None of your silly man foolishness is going to stop me."

She swept up the big tin and went out the door with it. We heard her on the steps, and a few seconds later the rattle of the cover of the garbage pail. We heard her on the steps again. She came in and went to the side bench where the dishpan was and began to scrub the pie tin. The way she acted, we might not have been in the room.

Father's face was getting red. He picked up his fork to begin eating and let it drop with a little clatter. He squirmed on his chair and kept taking quick side looks at her. She finished scrubbing the tin and went to the apple barrel and filled her wooden bowl with fat round ones. She sat by the stove and started peeling them. Father fished in a pocket and pulled out his old jackknife. He moved over to her, stepping softly. He reached out for an apple to help her.

She did not look up. But her voice caught him like she had flicked him with a whip. "Joe Starrett, don't you dare touch a one of these apples."

He was sheepish as he returned to his chair. Then he was downright mad. He grabbed his knife and fork and dug into the food on his plate, taking big bites and chewing vigorously. There was nothing for our visitor and me to do but follow his example. Maybe it was a good supper. I could not tell. The food was only something to put in your mouth. And when we finished, there was nothing to do but wait because mother was sitting by the stove, arms folded, staring at the wall, waiting herself for her pie to bake.

We three watched her in a quiet so tight that it hurt. We could not help it. We would try to look away and always our eyes would turn back to her. She did not appear to notice us. You might have said she had forgotten we were there.

She had not forgotten because as soon as she sensed that the pie was done, she lifted it out, cut four wide pieces, and put them on plates. The first two she set in front of the two men. The third one she set down for me. The last one she laid at her own place and she sat down in her own chair at the table. Her voice was still sharp.

"I'm sorry to keep you men waiting so long. Your pie is ready now."

Father inspected his portion like he was afraid of it. He needed to make a real effort to take his fork and lift a piece. He chewed on it and swallowed and he flipped his eyes sidewise at mother and back again quickly to look across the table at Shane. "That's prime pie," he said.

Shane raised a piece on his fork. He considered it closely. He put it in his mouth and chewed on it gravely. "Yes," he said. The quizzical expression on his face was so plain you could not possibly miss it. "Yes. That's the best bit of stump I ever tasted."

What could a silly remark like that mean? I had no time to wonder, for father and mother were acting so queer. They both stared at Shane and their mouths were sagging open. Then father snapped his shut and he chuckled and chuckled till he was swaying in his chair.

"By Godfrey, Marian, he's right. You've done it, too."

Mother stared from one to the other of them. Her pinched look faded and her cheeks were flushed and her eyes were soft and warm as they should be, and she was laughing so that the tears came. And all of us were pitching into that pie, and the one thing wrong in the whole world was that there was not enough of it.

4

The sun was already well up the sky when I awakened the next morning. I had been a long time getting to sleep because my mind was full of the day's excitement and shifting moods. I could not straighten out in my mind the way the grown folks had behaved, the way things that did not really matter so much had become so important to them.

I had lain in my bed thinking of our visitor out in the bunk in the barn. It scarce seemed possible that he was the same man I had first seen, stern and chilling in his dark solitude, riding up our road. Something in father, something not of words or of actions but of the essential substance of the human spirit, had reached out and spoken to him and he had replied to it and had unlocked a part of himself to us. He was far off and unapproachable at times even when he was right there with you. Yet somehow he was closer, too, than my uncle, mother's brother, had been when he visited us the summer before.

I had been thinking, too, of the effect he had on father and mother. They were more alive, more vibrant, like they wanted to show more what they were, when they were with him. I could appreciate that because I felt the same way myself. But it puzzled me that a man so deep and vital in his own being, so ready to respond to father, should be riding a lone trail out of a closed and guarded past.

I realized with a jolt how late it was. The door to my little room was closed. Mother must have closed it so I could sleep undisturbed. I was frantic that the others might have finished breakfast and that our visitor was gone and I had missed him. I pulled on my clothes, not even bothering with buttons, and ran to the door.

They were still at the table. Father was fussing with his pipe. Mother and Shane were working on a last round of coffee. All three of them were subdued and quiet. They stared at me as I burst out of my room.

"My heavens," said mother. "You came in here like something was after you. What's the matter?"

"I just thought," I blurted out, nodding at our visitor, "that maybe he had ridden off and forgotten me."

Shane shook his head slightly, looking straight at me. "I wouldn't forget you, Bob." He pulled himself up a little in his chair. He turned to mother and his voice took on a bantering tone. "And I wouldn't forget your cooking, ma'am. If you begin having a special lot of people passing by at mealtimes, that'll be because a grateful man has been boasting of your flannel cakes all along the road."

"Now there's an idea," struck in father as if he was glad to find something safe to talk about. "We'll turn this place into a boarding house. Marian'll fill folks full of her meals and I'll fill my pockets full of their money. That hits me as a mighty convenient arrangement."

Mother sniffed at him. But she was pleased at their talk and she was smiling as they kept on playing with the idea while she stirred me up my breakfast. She came right back at them, threatening to take father at his word and make him spend all his time peeling potatoes and washing dishes. They were enjoying themselves even though I could feel a bit of constraint behind the easy joshing. It was remarkable, too, how natural it was to have this Shane sitting there and joining in almost like he was a member of the family. There was none of the awkwardness some visitors always brought with them. You did feel you ought to be on your good behavior with him, a mite extra careful about your manners and your speech. But not stiffly so. Just quiet and friendly about it.

He stood up at last and I knew he was going to ride away from us and I wanted desperately to stop him. Father did it for me.

"You certainly are a man for being in a hurry. Sit down, Shane. I've a question to ask you."

Father was suddenly very serious. Shane, standing there, was as suddenly withdrawn into a distant alertness. But he dropped back into his chair.

Father looked directly at him. "Are you running away from anything?"

Shane stared at the plate in front of him for a long moment. It seemed to me that a shade of sadness passed over him. Then he raised his eyes and looked directly at father.

"No. I'm not running away from anything. Not in the way you mean."

"Good." Father stooped forward and stabbed at the table with a forefinger for emphasis. "Look, Shane. I'm not a rancher. Now you've seen my place, you know that. I'm a farmer. Something of a stockman, maybe. But really a farmer. That's what I decided to be when I quit punching cattle for another man's money. That's what I want to be and I'm proud of it. I've made a fair start. This outfit isn't as big as I hope to have it some day. But there's more work here already than one man can handle if it's to be done right. The young fellow I had ran out on me after he tangled with a couple of Fletcher's boys in town one day." Father was talking fast and he paused to draw breath.

Shane had been watching him intently. He moved his head to look out the window over the valley to the mountains marching along the horizon. "It's always the same," he murmured. He was sort of talking to himself. "The old ways die hard." He looked at mother and then at me, and as his eyes came back to father he seemed to have decided something that had been troubling him. "So Fletcher's crowding you," he said gently.

Father snorted. "I don't crowd easy. But I've got a job to do here and it's too big for one man, even for me. And none of the strays that drift up this way are worth a damn."

"Yes?" Shane said. His eyes were crinkling again, and he was one of us again and waiting.

"Will you stick here awhile and help me get things in shape for the winter?"

Shane rose to his feet. He loomed up taller across the table than I had thought him. "I never figured to be a farmer, Starrett. I would have laughed at the notion a few days ago. All the same, you've hired yourself a hand." He and father were looking at each other in a way that showed they were saying things words could never cover. Shane snapped it by swinging toward mother. "And I'll rate your cooking, ma'am, wages enough."

Father slapped his hands on his knees. "You'll get good wages and you'll earn 'em. First off, now, why don't you drop into town and get some work clothes. Try Sam Grafton's store. Tell him to put it on my bill."

Shane was already at the door. "I'll buy my own," he said, and was gone.

Father was so pleased he could not sit still. He jumped up and whirled mother around. "Marian, the sun's shining mighty bright at last. We've got ourselves a man."

"But, Joe, are you sure what you're doing? What kind of work can a man like that do? Oh, I know he stood right up to you with that stump. But that was something special. He's been used to good living and plenty of money. You can tell that. He said himself he doesn't know anything about farming."

"Neither did I when I started here. What a man knows isn't important. It's what he is that counts. I'll bet you that one was a cowpuncher when he was younger and a tophand too. Anything he does will be done right. You watch. In a week he'll be making even me hump or he'll be bossing the place."

"Perhaps."

"No perhapsing about it. Did you notice how he took it when I told him about Fletcher's boys and young Morley? That's what fetched him. He knows I'm in a spot and he's not the man to leave me there. Nobody'll push him around or scare him away. He's my kind of a man."

"Why, Joe Starrett. He isn't like you at all. He's smaller and he looks different and his clothes are different and he talks different. I know he's lived different."

"Huh?" Father was surprised. "I wasn't talking about things like that."

Shane came back with a pair of dungaree pants, a flannel shirt, stout work shoes, and a good, serviceable Stetson. He disappeared into the barn and emerged a few moments later in his new clothes, leading his horse unsaddled. At the pasture gate he slipped off the halter, turned the horse in with a hearty slap, and tossed the halter to me.

"Take care of a horse, Bob, and it will take care of you. This one now has brought me better than a thousand miles in the last few weeks." And he was striding away to join father, who was ditching the field out past the growing corn where the ground was rich but marshy and would not be worth much till it was properly drained. I watched him swinging through the rows of young corn, no longer a dark stranger but part of the place, a farmer like father and me.

Only he was not a farmer and never really could be. It was not three days before you saw that he could stay right beside father in any kind of work. Show him what needed to be done and he could do it, and like as not would figure out a better way of getting it done. He never shirked the meanest task. He was ever ready to take the hard end of any chore. Yet you always felt in some indefinable fashion that he was a man apart.

There were times when he would stop and look off at the mountains and then down at himself and any tool he happened to have in his hands as if in wry amusement at what he was doing. You had no impression that he thought himself too good for the work or did not like it. He was just different. He was shaped in some firm forging of past circumstance for other things.

For all his slim build he was plenty rugged. His slenderness could fool you at first. But when you saw him close in action, you saw that he was solid, compact, that there was no waste weight on his frame just as there was no waste effort in his smooth, flowing motion. What he lacked alongside father in size and strength, he made up in quickness of movement, in instinctive coordination of mind and muscle, and in that sudden fierce energy that had burned in him when the old stump tried to topple back on him. Mostly this last slept in him, not needed while he went easily through the day's routine. But when a call came, it could flame forward with a driving intensity that never failed to frighten me.

I would be frightened, as I had tried to explain to mother, not at Shane himself, but at the suggestion it always gave me of things in the human equation beyond my comprehension. At such times there would be a concentration in him, a singleness of dedication to the instant need, that seemed to me at once wonderful and disturbing. And then he would be again the quiet, steady man who shared with father my boy's allegiance.

I was beginning to feel my oats about then, proud of myself for being able to lick Ollie Johnson at the next place down the road. Fighting, boy style, was much in my mind.

Once, when father and I were alone, I asked him: "Could you beat Shane? In a fight, I mean."

"Son, that's a tough question. If I had to, I might do it. But, by Godfrey, I'd hate to try it. Some men just plain have dynamite inside them, and he's one. I'll tell you, though, I've never met a man I'd rather have more on my side in any kind of trouble."

I could understand that and it satisfied me. But there were things about Shane I could not understand. When he came in to the first meal after he agreed to stay on with us, he went to the chair that had always been father's and stood beside it waiting for the rest of us to take the other places. Mother was surprised and somewhat annoyed. She started to say something. Father quieted her with a warning glance. He walked to the chair across from Shane and sat down like this was the right and natural spot for him and afterwards he and Shane always used these same places.

I could not see any reason for the shift until the first time one of our homestead neighbors knocked on the door while we were eating and came straight on in as most of them usually did. Then I suddenly realized that Shane was sitting opposite the door where he could directly confront anyone coming through it. I could see that was the way he wanted it to be. But I could not understand why he wanted it that way.

In the evenings after supper when he was talking lazily with us, he would never sit by a window. Out on the porch he would always face the road. He liked to have a wall behind him and not just to lean against. No matter where he was, away from the table, before sitting down he would swing his chair into position, back to the nearest wall, not making any show, simply putting it there and bending into it in one easy motion. He did not even seem to be aware that this was unusual. It was part of his fixed alertness. He always wanted to know everything happening around him.

This alertness could be noted, too, in the watch he kept, without appearing to make any special effort, on every approach to our place. He knew first when anyone was moving along the road and he would stop whatever he was doing to study carefully any passing rider.

We often had company in the evenings, for the other homesteaders regarded father as their leader and would drop in to discuss their affairs with him. They were interesting men in their own fashions, a various assortment. But Shane was not anxious to meet people. He would share little in their talk. With us he spoke freely enough. We were, in some subtle way, his folks. Though we had taken him in, you had the feeling that he had adopted us. But with others he was reserved; courteous and softspoken, yet withdrawn beyond a line of his own making.

These things puzzled me and not me alone. The people in town and those who rode or drove in pretty regularly were all curious about him. It was a wonder how quickly everyone in the valley, and even on the ranches out in the open country, knew that he was working with father.

They were not sure they liked having him in their neighborhood. Ledyard had told some tall tale about what happened at our place that made them stare sharply at Shane whenever they had a chance. But they must have had their own measure of Ledyard, for they did not take his story too straight. They just could not really make up their minds about Shane and it seemed to worry them.

More than once, when I was with Ollie Johnson on the way to our favorite fishing hole the other side of town, I heard men arguing about him in front of Mr. Grafton's store. "He's like one of these here slow-burning fuses," I heard an old mule-skinner say one day. "Quiet and no sputtering. So quiet you forget it's burning. Then it sets off one hell of a blow-off of trouble when it touches powder. That's him. And there's been trouble brewing in this valley for a long spell now. Maybe it'll be good when it comes. Maybe it'll be bad. You just can't tell." And that puzzled me too.

What puzzled me most, though, was something it took me nearly two weeks to appreciate. And yet it was the most striking thing of all. Shane carried no gun.

In those days guns were as familiar all through the Territory as boots and saddles. They were not used much in the valley except for occasional hunting. But they were always in evidence. Most men did not feel fully dressed without one.

We homesteaders went in mostly for rifles and shotguns when we had any shooting to do. A pistol slapping on the hip was a nuisance for a farmer. Still every man had his cartridge belt and holstered Colt to be worn when he was not working or loafing around the house. Father buckled his on whenever he rode off on any trip, even just into town, as much out of habit, I guess, as anything else.

But this Shane never carried a gun. And that was a peculiar thing because he had a gun.

I saw it once. I saw it when I was alone in the barn one day and I spotted his saddle-roll lying on his bunk. Usually he kept it carefully put away underneath. He must have forgotten it this time, for it was there in the open by the pillow. I reached to sort of feel it—and I felt the gun inside. No one was near, so I unfastened the straps and unrolled the blankets. There it was, the most beautiful-looking weapon I ever saw. Beautiful and deadly-looking.

The holster and filled cartridge belt were of the same soft black leather as the boots tucked under the bunk, tooled in the same intricate design. I knew enough to know that the gun was a single-action Colt, the same model as the Regular Army issue that was the favorite of all men in those days and that oldtimers used to say was the finest pistol ever made.

This was the same model. But this was no Army gun. It was black, almost blue black, with the darkness not in any enamel but in the metal itself. The grip was clear on the outer curve, shaped to the fingers on the inner curve, and two ivory plates were set into it with exquisite skill, one on each side.

The smooth invitation of it tempted your grasp. I took hold and pulled the gun out of the holster. It came so easily that I could hardly believe it was there in my hand. Heavy like father's, it was somehow much easier to handle.

You held it up to aiming level and it seemed to balance itself into your hand.

It was clean and polished and oiled. The empty cylinder, when I released the catch and flicked it, spun swiftly and noiselessly. I was surprised to see that the front sight was gone, the barrel smooth right down to the end, and that the hammer had been filed to a sharp point.

Why should a man do that to a gun? Why should a man with a gun like that refuse to wear it and show it off? And then, staring at that dark and deadly efficiency, I was again suddenly chilled, and I quickly put everything back exactly as before and hurried out into the sun.

The first chance I tried to tell father about it. "Father," I said, all excited, "do you know what Shane has rolled up in his blankets?"

"Probably a gun."

"But—but how did you know? Have you seen it?"

"No. That's what he would have."

I was all mixed up. "Well, why doesn't he ever carry it? Do you suppose maybe it's because he doesn't know how to use it very well?"

Father chuckled like I had made a joke. "Son, I wouldn't be surprised if he could take that gun and shoot the buttons off your shirt with you awearing it and all you'd feel would be a breeze."

"Gosh agorry! Why does he keep it hidden in the barn then?"

"I don't know. Not exactly."

"Why don't you ask him?"

Father looked straight at me, very serious. "That's one question I'll never ask him. And don't you ever say anything to him about it. There are some things you don't ask a man. Not if you respect him. He's entitled to stake his claim to what he considers private to himself alone. But you can take my word for it, Bob, that when a man like Shane doesn't want to tote a gun you can bet your shirt, buttons and all, he's got a mighty good reason."

That was that. I was still mixed up. But whenever father gave you his word on something, there was nothing more to be said. He never did that except when he knew he was right. I started to wander off.

"Bob."

"Yes, father."

"Listen to me, son. Don't get to liking Shane too much."

"Why not? Is there anything wrong with him?"

"No-o-o-o. There's nothing wrong about Shane. Nothing you could put that way. There's more right about him than most any man you're ever likely to meet. But—" Father was throwing around for what to say. "But he's fiddle-footed. Remember. He said so himself. He'll be moving on one of these days and then you'll be all upset if you get to liking him too much."

That was not what father really meant. But that was what he wanted me to think. So I did not ask any more questions.

5

THE WEEKS went rocking past, and soon it did not seem possible that there ever had been a time when Shane was not with us. He and father worked together more like partners than boss and hired man. The amount they could get through in a day was a marvel. The ditching father had reckoned would take him most of the summer was done in less than a month. The loft was finished and the first cutting of alfalfa stowed away.

We would have enough fodder to carry a few more young steers through the winter for fattening next summer, so father rode out of the valley and all the way to the ranch where he worked once and came back herding a half-dozen more. He was gone two days. He came back to find that Shane, while he was gone, had knocked out the end of the corral and posted a new section making it half again as big.

"Now we can really get going next year," Shane said as father sat on his horse staring at the corral like he could not quite believe what he saw. "We ought to get enough hay off that new field to help us carry forty head."

"Oho!" said father. "So we can get going. And we ought to get enough hay." He was pleased as could be because he was scowling at Shane the way he did at me when he was tickled silly over something I had done and did not want to let on that he was. He jumped off his horse and hurried up to the house where mother was standing on the porch.

"Marian," he demanded right off, waving at the corral, "whose idea was that?"

"Well-l-l," she said, "Shane suggested it." Then she added slyly, "But I told him to go ahead."

"That's right." Shane had come up beside him. "She rode me like she had spurs to get it done by today. Kind of a present. It's your wedding anniversary."

"Well, I'll be damned," said father. "So it is." He stared foolishly at one and then the other of them. With Shane there watching, he hopped on the porch and gave mother a kiss. I was embarrassed for him and I turned away—and hopped about a foot myself.

"Hey! Those steers are running away!"

The grown folks had forgotten about them. All six were wandering up the road, straggling and separating. Shane, that soft-spoken man, let out a whoop you might have heard halfway to town and ran to father's horse, putting his hands on the saddle and vaulting into it. He fairly lifted the horse into a gallop in one leap and that old cowpony of father's lit out after those steers like this was fun. By the time father reached the corral gate, Shane had the runaways in a compact bunch and padding back at a trot. He dropped them through the gateway neat as pie.

He was tall and straight in the saddle the few seconds it took father to close the gate. He and the horse were blowing a bit and both of them were perky and proud.

"It's been ten years," he said, "since I did anything like that."

Father grinned at him. "Shane, if I didn't know better, I'd say you were a faker. There's still a lot of kid in you."

The first real smile I had seen yet flashed across Shane's face. "Maybe. Maybe there is at that."

I think that was the happiest summer of my life.

The only shadow over our valley, the recurrent trouble between Fletcher and us homesteaders, seemed to have faded away. Fletcher himself was gone most of those months. He had gone to Fort Bennett in Dakota and even on East to Washington, so we heard, trying to get a contract to supply beef to the Indian agent at Standing Rock, the big Sioux reservation over beyond the Black Hills. Except for his foreman, Morgan, and several surly older men, his hands were young, easy-going cowboys who made a lot of noise in town once in a while but rarely did any harm and even then only in high spirits. We liked them— when Fletcher was not there driving them into harassing us in constant shrewd ways. Now, with him away, they kept to the other side of the river and did not bother us. Sometimes, riding in sight on the other bank, they might even wave to us in their rollicking fashion.

Until Shane came, they had been my heroes. Father, of course, was special all to himself. There could never be anyone quite to match him. I wanted to be like him, just as he was. But first I wanted, as he had done, to ride the range, to have my own string of ponies and take part in an all-brand round-up and in a big cattle drive and dash into strange towns with just such a rollicking crew and with a season's pay jingling in my pockets.

Now I was not so sure. I wanted more and more to be like Shane, like the man I imagined he was in the past fenced off so securely. I had to imagine most of it. He would never speak of it, not in any way at all. Even his name remained mysterious. Just Shane. Nothing else. We never knew whether that was his first name or last name or, indeed, any name that came from his family. "Call me

Shane," he said, and that was all he ever said. But I conjured up all manner of adventures for him, not tied to any particular time or place, seeing him as a slim and dark and dashing figure coolly passing through perils that would overcome a lesser man.

I would listen in what was closely akin to worship while my two men, father and Shane, argued long and amiably about the cattle business. They would wrangle over methods of feeding and bringing steers up to top weight. But they were agreed that controlled breeding was better than open range running and that improvement of stock was needed even if that meant spending big money on imported bulls. And they would speculate about the chances of a railroad spur ever reaching the valley, so you could ship direct without thinning good meat off your cattle driving them to market.

It was plain that Shane was beginning to enjoy living with us and working the place. Little by little the tension in him was fading out. He was still alert and watchful, instinct with that unfailing awareness of everything about him. I came to realize that this was inherent in him, not learned or acquired, simply a part of his natural being. But the sharp extra edge of conscious alertness, almost of expectancy of some unknown trouble always waiting, was wearing away.

Yet why was he sometimes so strange and stricken in his own secret bitterness? Like the time I was playing with a gun Mr. Grafton gave me, an old frontier model Colt with a cracked barrel someone had turned in at the store.

I had rigged a holster out of a torn chunk of oilcloth and a belt of rope. I was stalking around near the barn, whirling every few steps to pick off a skulking Indian, when I saw Shane watching me from the barn door. I stopped short, thinking of that beautiful gun under his bunk and afraid he would make fun of me and my sorry old broken pistol. Instead he looked gravely at me.

"How many you knocked over so far, Bob?"

Could I ever repay the man? My gun was a shining new weapon, my hand steady as a rock as I drew a bead on another one.

"That makes seven."

"Indians or timber wolves?"

"Indians. Big ones."

"Better leave a few for the other scouts," he said gently. "It wouldn't do to make them jealous. And look here, Bob. You're not doing that quite right."

He sat down on an upturned crate and beckoned me over. "Your holster's too low. Don't let it drag full arm's length. Have it just below the hip, so the grip is about halfway between your wrist and elbow when the arm's hanging limp. You can take the gun then as your hand's coming up and there's still room to clear the holster without having to lift the gun too high."

"Gosh agorry! Is that the way the real gunfighters do?"

A queer light flickered in his eyes and was gone. "No. Not all of them. Most have their own tricks. One likes a shoulder holster; another packs his gun in his pants belt. Some carry two guns, but that's a show-off stunt and a waste of weight. One's enough, if you know how to use it. I've even seen a man have a tight holster with an open end and fastened on a little swivel to the belt. He didn't have to pull the gun then. Just swung up the barrel and blazed away from the hip. That's mighty fast for close work and a big target. But it's not certain past ten or fifteen paces and no good at all for putting your shot right where you want it. The way I'm telling you is as good as any and better than most. And another thing—"

He reached and took the gun. Suddenly, as for the first time, I was aware of his hands. They were broad and strong, but not heavy and fleshy like father's. The fingers were long and square on the ends. It was funny how, touching the gun, the hands seemed to have an intelligence all their own, a sure movement that needed no guidance of thought.

His right hand closed around the grip and you knew at once it was doing what it had been created for. He hefted the old gun, letting it lie loosely in the hand. Then the fingers tightened and the thumb toyed with the hammer, testing the play of it.

While I gaped at him, he tossed it swiftly in the air and caught it in his left hand and in the instant of catching, it nestled snugly into this hand too. He tossed it again, high this time and spinning end over end, and as it came down, his right hand flicked forward and took it. The forefinger slipped through the trigger guard and the gun spun, coming up into firing position in the one unbroken motion. With him that old pistol seemed alive, not an inanimate and rusting metal object, but an extension of the man himself.

"If it's speed you're after, Bob, don't split the move into parts. Don't pull, cock, aim, and fire. Slip back the hammer as you bring the gun up and squeeze the trigger the second it's up level."

"How do you aim it, then? How do you get a sight on it?"

"No need to. Learn to hold it so the barrel's right in line with the fingers if they were out straight. You won't have to waste time bringing it high to take a sight. Just point it, low and quick and easy, like pointing a finger."

Like pointing a finger. As the words came, he was doing it. The old gun was bearing on some target over by the corral and the hammer was clicking at the empty cylinder. Then the hand around the gun whitened and the fingers slowly opened and the gun fell to the ground. The hand sank to his side, stiff and awkward. He raised his head and the mouth was a bitter gash in his face. His eyes were fastened on the mountains climbing in the distance.

"Shane! Shane! What's the matter?"

He did not hear me. He was back somewhere along the dark trail of the past.

He took a deep breath, and I could see the effort run through him as he dragged himself into the present and a realization of a boy staring at him. He beckoned to me to pick up the gun. When I did he leaned forward and spoke earnestly.

"Listen, Bob. A gun is just a tool. No better and no worse than any other tool, a shovel—or an axe or a saddle or a stove or anything. Think of it always that way. A gun is as good—and as bad—as the man who carries it. Remember that."

He stood up and strode off into the fields and I knew he

wanted to be alone. I remembered what he said all right, tucked away unforgettably in my mind. But in those days I remembered more the way he handled the gun and the advice he gave me about using it. I would practice with it and think of the time when I could have one that would really shoot.

And then the summer was over. School began again and the days were growing shorter and the first cutting edge of cold was creeping down from the mountains.

6

MORE THAN THE SUMMER was over. The season of friendship in our valley was fading with the sun's warmth. Fletcher was back and he had his contract. He was talking in town that he would need the whole range again. The homesteaders would have to go.

He was a reasonable man, he was saying in his smooth way, and he would pay a fair price for any improvements they had put in. But we knew what Luke Fletcher would call a fair price. And we had no intention of leaving. The land was ours by right of settlement, guaranteed by the government. Only we knew, too, how faraway the government was from our valley way up there in the Territory.

The nearest marshal was a good hundred miles away. We did not even have a sheriff in our town. There never had been any reason for one. When folks had any lawing to do, they would head for Sheridan, nearly a full day's ride away. Our town was small, not even organized as a town. It was growing, but it was still not much more than a roadside settlement.

The first people there were three or four miners who had come prospecting after the blow-up of the Big Horn

Mining Association about twenty years before, and had found gold traces leading to a moderate vein in the jutting rocks that partially closed off the valley where it edged into the plain. You could not have called it a strike, for others that followed were soon disappointed. Those first few, however, had done fairly well and had brought in their families and a number of helpers.

Then a stage and freighting line had picked the site for a relay post. That meant a place where you could get drinks as well as horses, and before long the cowboys from the ranches out on the plain and Fletcher's spread in the valley were drifting in of an evening. With us homesteaders coming now, one or two more almost every season, the town was taking shape. Already there were several stores, a harness and blacksmith shop, and nearly a dozen houses. Just the year before, the men had put together a one-room schoolhouse.

Sam Grafton's place was the biggest. He had a general store with several rooms for living quarters back of it in one half of his rambling building, a saloon with a long bar and tables for cards and the like in the other half. Upstairs he had some rooms he rented to stray drummers or anyone else stranded overnight. He acted as our postmaster, an elderly man, a close bargainer but honest in all his dealings. Sometimes he served as a sort of magistrate in minor disputes. His wife was dead. His daughter Jane kept house for him and was our schoolteacher when school was in session.

Even if we had had a sheriff, he would have been Fletcher's man. Fletcher was the power in the valley in those days. We homesteaders had been around only a few years and the other people still thought of us as there by his sufferance. He had been running cattle through the whole valley at the time the miners arrived, having bought or bulldozed out the few small ranchers there ahead of him. A series of bad years working up to the dry summer and terrible winter of '86 had cut his herds about the time the first of the homesteaders moved in and he had not objected too much. But now there were seven of us in all and the number rising each year.

It was a certain thing, father used to say, that the town

would grow and swing our way. Mr. Grafton knew that too, I guess, but he was a careful man who never let thoughts about the future interfere with present business. The others were the kind to veer with the prevailing wind. Fletcher was the big man in the valley, so they looked up to him and tolerated us. Led to it, they probably would have helped him run us out. With him out of the way, they would just as willingly accept us. And Fletcher was back, with a contract in his pocket, wanting his full range again.

There was a hurried counsel in our house soon as the news was around. Our neighbor toward town, Lew Johnson, who heard it in Grafton's store, spread the word and arrived first. He was followed by Henry Shipstead, who had the place next to him, the closest to town. These two had been the original homesteaders, staking out their hundred and eighties two years before the drought and riding out Fletcher's annoyance until the cut in his herds gave him other worries. They were solid, dependable men, old-line farmers who had come West from Iowa.

You could not say quite as much for the rest, straggling in at intervals. James Lewis and Ed Howells were two middle-aged cowhands who had grown dissatisfied and tagged father into the valley, coming pretty much on his example. Lacking his energy and drive, they had not done too well and could be easily discouraged.

Frank Torrey from farther up the valley was a nervous, fidgety man with a querulous wife and a string of dirty kids growing longer every year. He was always talking about pulling up stakes and heading for California. But he had a stubborn streak in him, and he was always saying, too, that he'd be damned if he'd make tracks just because some big-hatted rancher wanted him to.

Ernie Wright, who had the last stand up the valley butting out into the range still used by Fletcher, was probably the weakest of the lot. Not in any physical way. He was a husky, likable man, so dark-complected that there were rumors he was part Indian. He was always singing and telling tall stories. But he would be off hunting when he should be working and he had a quick temper that would trap him into doing fool things without taking thought.

He was as serious as the rest of them that night. Mr. Grafton had said that this time Fletcher meant business. His contract called for all the beef he could drive in the next five years and he was determined to push the chance to the limit.

"But what can he do?" asked Frank Torrey. "The land's ours as long as we live on it and we get title in three years. Some of you fellows have already proved up."

"He won't really make trouble," chimed in James Lewis. "Fletcher's never been the shooting kind. He's a good talker, but talk can't hurt us." Several of the others nodded. Johnson and Shipstead did not seem to be so sure. Father had not said anything yet and they all looked at him.

"Jim's right," he admitted. "Fletcher hasn't ever let his boys get careless thataway. Not yet anyhow. That ain't saying he wouldn't, if there wasn't any other way. There's a hard streak in him. But he won't get real tough for a while. I don't figure he'll start moving cattle in now till spring. My guess is he'll try putting pressure on us this fall and winter, see if he can wear us down. He'll probably start right here. He doesn't like any of us. But he doesn't like me most."

"That's true." Ed Howells was expressing the unspoken verdict that father was their leader. "How do you figure he'll go about it?"

"My guess on that," father said—drawling now and smiling a grim little smile like he knew he was holding a good hole card in a tight game—"my guess on that is that he'll begin by trying to convince Shane here that it isn't healthy to be working with me."

"You mean the way he—" began Ernie Wright.

"Yes." Father cut him short. "I mean the way he did with young Morley."

I was peeping around the door of my little room. I saw Shane sitting off to one side, listening quietly as he had been right along. He did not seem the least bit surprised. He did not seem the least bit interested in finding out what had happened to young Morley. I knew what had. I had seen Morley come back from town, bruised and a beaten man, and gather his things and curse father for hiring him and ride away without once looking back.

Yet Shane sat there quietly as if what had happened to Morley had nothing to do with him. He simply did not care what it was. And then I understood why. It was because he was not Morley. He was Shane.

Father was right. In some strange fashion the feeling was abroad that Shane was a marked man. Attention was on him as a sort of symbol. By taking him on father had accepted in a way a challenge from the big ranch across the river. What had happened to Morley had been a warning and father had deliberately answered it. The long unpleasantness was sharpened now after the summer lull. The issue in our valley was plain and would in time have to be pushed to a showdown. If Shane could be driven out, there would be a break in the homestead ranks, a defeat going beyond the loss of a man into the realm of prestige and morale. It could be the crack in the dam that weakens the whole structure and finally lets through the flood.

The people in town were more curious than ever, not now so much about Shane's past as about what he might do if Fletcher tried any move against him. They would stop me and ask me questions when I was hurrying to and from school. I knew that father would not want me to say anything and I pretended that I did not know what they were talking about. But I used to watch Shane closely myself and wonder how all the slow-climbing tenseness in our valley could be so focused on one man and he seem to be so indifferent to it.

For of course he was aware of it. He never missed anything. Yet he went about his work as usual, smiling frequently now at me, bantering mother at mealtimes in his courteous manner, arguing amiably as before with father on plans for next year. The only thing that was different was that there appeared to be a lot of new activity across the river. It was surprising how often Fletcher's cowboys were finding jobs to do within view of our place.

Then one afternoon, when we were stowing away the second and last cutting of hay, one fork of the big tongs we were using to haul it up to the loft broke loose. "Have to get it welded in town," father said in disgust and began to hitch up the team.

Shane stared over the river where a cowboy was riding lazily back and forth by a bunch of cattle. "I'll take it in," he said.

Father looked at Shane and he looked across the way and he grinned. "All right. It's as good a time as any." He slapped down the final buckle and started for the house. "Just a minute and I'll be ready."

"Take it easy, Joe." Shane's voice was gentle, but it stopped father in his tracks. "I said I'll take it in."

Father whirled to face him. "Damn it all, man. Do you think I'd let you go alone? Suppose they—" He bit down on his own words. He wiped a hand slowly across his face and he said what I had never heard him say to any man. "I'm sorry," he said. "I should have known better." He stood there silently watching as Shane gathered up the reins and jumped to the wagon seat.

I was afraid father would stop me, so I waited till Shane was driving out of the lane. I ducked behind the barn, around the end of the corral, and hopped into the wagon going past. As I did, I saw the cowboy across the river spin his horse and ride rapidly off in the direction of the ranch-house.

Shane saw it, too, and it seemed to give him a grim amusement. He reached backwards and hauled me over the seat and sat me beside him.

"You Starretts like to mix into things." For a moment I thought he might send me back. Instead he grinned at me. "I'll buy you a jackknife when we hit town."

He did, a dandy big one with two blades and a corkscrew. After we left the tongs with the blacksmith and found the welding would take nearly an hour, I squatted on the steps on the long porch across the front of Grafton's building, busy whittling, while Shane stepped into the saloon side and ordered a drink. Will Atkey, Grafton's thin, sad-faced clerk and bartender, was behind the bar and several other men were loafing at one of the tables.

It was only a few moments before two cowboys came

galloping down the road. They slowed to a walk about fifty yards off and with a show of nonchalance ambled the rest of the way to Grafton's, dismounting and looping their reins over the rail in front. One of them I had seen often, a young fellow everyone called Chris, who had worked with Fletcher several years and was known for a gay manner and reckless courage. The other was new to me, a sallow, pinch-cheek man, not much older, who looked like he had crowded a lot of hard living into his years. He must have been one of the new hands Fletcher had been bringing into the valley since he got his contract.

They paid no attention to me. They stepped softly up on the porch and to the window of the saloon part of the building. As they peered through, Chris nodded and jerked his head toward the inside. The new man stiffened. He leaned closer for a better look. Abruptly he turned clear about and came right down past me and went over to his horse.

Chris was startled and hurried after him. They were both so intent they did not realize I was there. The new man was lifting the reins back over his horse's head when Chris caught his arm.

"What the hell?"

"I'm leaving."

"Huh? I don't get it."

"I'm leaving. Now. For good."

"Hey, listen. Do you know that guy?"

"I didn't say that. There ain't nobody can claim I said that. I'm leaving, that's all. You can tell Fletcher. This is a hell of a country up here anyhow."

Chris was getting mad. "I might have known," he said. "Scared, eh. Yellow."

Color rushed into the new man's sallow face. But he climbed on his horse and swung out from the rail. "You can call it that," he said flatly and started down the road, out of town, out of the valley.

Chris was standing still by the rail, shaking his head in wonderment. "Hell," he said to himself, "I'll brace him myself." He stalked up on the porch, into the saloon.

I dashed into the store side, over to the opening between the two big rooms. I crouched on a box just inside the store where I could hear everything and see most of the other room. It was long and fairly wide. The bar curved out from the opening and ran all the way along the inner wall to the back wall, which closed off a room Grafton used as an office. There was a row of windows on the far side, too high for anyone to look in from outside. A small stairway behind them led up to a sort of balcony across the back with doors opening into several little rooms.

Shane was leaning easily with one arm on the bar, his drink in his other hand, when Chris came to perhaps six feet away and called for a whiskey bottle and a glass. Chris pretended he did not notice Shane at first and bobbed his head in greeting to the men at the table. They were a pair of mule-skinners who made regular trips into the valley freighting in goods for Grafton and the other shops. I could have sworn that Shane, studying Chris in his effortless way, was somehow disappointed.

Chris waited until he had his whiskey and had gulped a stiff shot. Then he deliberately looked Shane over like he had just spotted him.

"Hello, farmer," he said. He said it as if he did not like farmers.

Shane regarded him with grave attention. "Speaking to me?" he asked mildly and finished his drink.

"Hell, there ain't nobody else standing there. Here, have a drink of this." Chris shoved his bottle along the bar. Shane poured himself a generous slug and raised it to his lips.

"I'll be damned," flipped Chris. "So you drink whiskey."

Shane tossed off the rest in his glass and set it down. "I've had better," he said, as friendly as could be. "But this will do."

Chris slapped his leather chaps with a loud smack. He turned to take in the other men. "Did you hear that? This farmer drinks whiskey! I didn't think these plow-pushing dirt-grubbers drank anything stronger than soda pop!"

"Some of us do," said Shane, friendly as before. Then he was no longer friendly and his voice was like winter frost.

"You've had your fun and it's mighty young fun. Now run home and tell Fletcher to send a grown-up man next time." He turned away and sang out to Will Atkey. "Do you have any soda pop? I'd like a bottle."

Will hesitated, looked kind of funny, and scuttled past me into the store room. He came back right away with a bottle of the pop Grafton kept there for us school kids. Chris was standing quiet, not so much mad, I would have said, as puzzled. It was as though they were playing some queer game and he was not sure of the next move. He sucked on his lower lip for a while. Then he snapped his mouth and began to look elaborately around the room, sniffing loudly.

"Hey, Will!" he called. "What's been happening in here? It smells. That ain't no clean cattleman smell. That's plain dirty barnyard." He stared at Shane. "You, farmer. What are you and Starrett raising out there? Pigs?"

Shane was just taking hold of the bottle Will had fetched him. His hand closed on it and the knuckles showed white. He moved slowly, almost unwillingly, to face Chris. Every line of his body was as taut as stretched whip-cord, was alive and somehow rich with an immense eagerness. There was that fierce concentration in him, filling him, blazing in his eyes. In that moment there was nothing in the room for him but that mocking man only a few feet away.

The big room was so quiet the stillness fairly hurt. Chris stepped back involuntarily, one pace, two, then pulled up erect. And still nothing happened. The lean muscles along the sides of Shane's jaw were ridged like rock.

Then the breath, pent in him, broke the stillness with a soft sound as it left his lungs. He looked away from Chris, past him, over the tops of the swinging doors beyond, over the roof of the shed across the road, on into the distance where the mountains loomed in their own unending loneliness. Quietly he walked, the bottle forgotten in his hand, so close by Chris as almost to brush him yet apparently not even seeing him, through the doors and was gone.

I heard a sigh of relief near me. Mr. Grafton had come up from somewhere behind me. He was watching Chris with a strange, ironic quirk at his mouth corners. Chris was trying not to look pleased with himself. But he swaggered as he went to the doors and peered over them.

"You saw it, Will," he called over his shoulder. "He walked out on me." Chris pushed up his hat and rolled back on his heels and laughed. "With a bottle of soda pop too!" He was still laughing as he went out and we heard him ride away.

"That boy's a fool," Mr. Grafton muttered.

Will Atkey came sidling over to Mr. Grafton. "I never pegged Shane for a play like that," he said.

"He was afraid, Will."

"Yeah. That's what was so funny. I would've guessed he could take Chris."

Mr. Grafton looked at Will as he did often, like he was a little sorry for him. "No, Will. He wasn't afraid of Chris. He was afraid of himself." Mr. Grafton was thoughtful and perhaps sad too. "There's trouble ahead, Will. The worst trouble we've ever had."

He noticed me, realizing my presence. "Better skip along, Bob, and find your friend. Do you think he got that bottle for himself?"

True enough, Shane had it waiting for me at the blacksmith shop. Cherry pop, the kind I favored most. But I could not enjoy it much. Shane was so silent and stern. He had slipped back into the dark mood that was on him when he first came riding up our road. I did not dare say anything. Only once did he speak to me and I knew he did not expect me to understand or to answer.

"Why should a man be smashed because he has courage and does what he's told? Life's a dirty business, Bob. I could like that boy." And he turned inward again to his own thoughts and stayed the same until we had loaded the tongs in the wagon and were well started home. Then the closer we came, the more cheerful he was. By the time we swung in toward the barn, he was the way I wanted him again, crinkling his eyes at me and gravely joshing me about the Indians I would scalp with my new knife.

Father popped out the barn door so quick you could tell he had been itching for us to return. He was busting with curiosity, but he would not come straight out with a question to Shane. He tackled me instead.

"See any of your cowboy heroes in town?"

Shane cut in ahead of me. "One of Fletcher's crew chased us in to pay his respects."

"No," I said, proud of my information. "There was two of them."

"Two?" Shane said it. Father was the one who was not surprised. "What did the other one do?"

"He went up on the porch and looked in the window where you were and came right back down and rode off."

"Back to the ranch?"

"The other way. He said he was leaving for good."

Father and Shane looked at each other. Father was smiling. "One down and you didn't even know it. What did you do to the other?"

"Nothing. He passed a few remarks about farmers. I went back to the blacksmith shop."

Father repeated it, spacing the words like there might be meanings between them. "You—went—back—to—the—blacksmith—shop."

I was worried that he must be thinking what Will Atkey did. Then I knew nothing like that had even entered his head. He switched to me. "Who was it?"

"It was Chris."

Father was smiling again. He had not been there but he had the whole thing clear. "Fletcher was right to send two. Young ones like Chris need to hunt in pairs or they might get hurt." He chuckled in a sort of wry amusement. "Chris must have been considerable surprised when the other fellow skipped. And more when you walked out. It was too bad the other one didn't stick around."

"Yes," Shane said, "it was."

The way he said it sobered father. "I hadn't thought of that. Chris is just cocky enough to take it wrong. That can make things plenty unpleasant."

"Yes," Shane said again, "it can."

7

IT WAS JUST as father and Shane had said. The story Chris told was common knowledge all through the valley before the sun set the next day and the story grew in the telling. Fletcher had an advantage now and he was quick to push it. He and his foreman, Morgan, a broad slab of a man with flattened face and head small in proportion to great sloping shoulders, were shrewd at things like this and they kept their men primed to rowel us homesteaders at every chance.

They took to using the upper ford, up above Ernie Wright's stand, and riding down the road past our places every time they had an excuse for going to town. They would go by slowly, looking everything over with insolent interest and passing remarks for our benefit.

The same week, maybe three days later, a covey of them came riding by while father was putting a new hinge on the corral gate. They acted like they were too busy staring over our land to see him there close.

"Wonder where Starrett keeps the critters," said one of them. "I don't see a pig in sight."

"But I can smell 'em!" shouted another one. With that they all began to laugh and whoop and holler and went tearing off, kicking up a lot of dust and leaving father with a tightness around his mouth that was not there before.

They were impartial with attentions like that. They would hand them out anywhere along the line an opportunity offered. But they liked best to catch father within earshot and burn him with their sarcasm.

It was crude. It was coarse. I thought it silly for grown

men to act that way. But it was effective. Shane, as self-sufficient as the mountains, could ignore it. Father, while it galled him, could keep it from getting him. The other homesteaders, though, could not help being irritated and showing they felt insulted. It roughed their nerves and made them angry and restless. They did not know Shane as father and I did. They were not sure there might not be some truth in the big talk Chris was making.

Things became so bad they could not go into Grafton's store without someone singing out for soda pop. And wherever they went, the conversation near by always snuck around somehow to pigs. You could sense the contempt building up in town, in people who used to be neutral, not taking sides.

The effect showed, too, in the attitude our neighbors now had toward Shane. They were constrained when they called to see father and Shane was there. They resented that he was linked to them. And as a result their opinion of father was changing.

That was what finally drove Shane. He did not mind what they thought of him. Since his session with Chris he seemed to have won a kind of inner peace. He was as alert and watchful as ever, but there was a serenity in him that had erased entirely the old tension. I think he did not care what anyone anywhere thought of him. Except us, his folks. And he knew that with us he was one of us, unchangeable and always.

But he did care what they thought of father. He was standing silently on the porch the night Ernie Wright and Henry Shipstead were arguing with father in the kitchen.

"I can't stomach much more," Ernie Wright was saying. "You know the trouble I've had with those blasted cowboys cutting my fence. Today a couple of them rode over and helped me repair a piece. Helped me, damn them! Waited till we were through, then said Fletcher didn't want any of my pigs getting loose and mixing with his cattle. My pigs! There ain't a pig in this whole valley and they know it. I'm sick of the word."

Father made it worse by chuckling. Grim, maybe, yet still a chuckle. "Sounds like one of Morgan's ideas. He's smart. Mean, but—"

Henry Shipstead would not let him finish. "This is nothing to laugh at, Joe. You least of all. Damn it, man, I'm beginning to doubt your judgment. None of us can keep our heads up around here any more. Just a while ago I was in Grafton's and Chris was there blowing high about your Shane must be thirsty because he's so scared he hasn't been in town lately for his soda pop."

Both of them were hammering at father now. He was sitting back, saying nothing, his face clouding.

"You can't dodge it, Joe." This was Wright. "Your man's responsible. You can try explaining all night, but you can't change the facts. Chris braced him for a fight and he ducked out—and left us stuck with those stinking pigs."

"You know as well as I do what Fletcher's doing," growled Henry Shipstead. "He's pushing us with this and he won't let up till one of us gets enough and makes a fool play and starts something so he can move in and finish it."

"Fool play or not," said Ernie Wright. "I've had all I can take. The next time one of those—"

Father stopped him with a hand up for silence. "Listen. What's that?"

It was a horse picking up speed and tearing down our lane into the road. Father was at the door in a single jump, peering out.

The others were close behind him. "Shane?"

Father nodded. He was muttering under his breath. As I watched from the doorway of my little room, I could see that his eyes were bright and dancing. He was calling Shane names, cursing him, softly, fluently. He came back to his chair and grinned at the other two. "That's Shane," he told them and the words meant more than they seemed to say. "All we can do now is wait."

They were a silent crew waiting. Mother got up from her sewing in the bedroom where she had been listening

as she always did and came into the kitchen and made up
a pot of coffee and they all sat there sipping at the hot stuff
and waiting.

It could not have been much more than twenty minutes
before we heard the horse again, coming swiftly and slew-
ing around to make the lane without slowing. There were
quick steps on the porch and Shane stood in the doorway.
He was breathing strongly and his face was hard. His mouth
was a thin line in the bleakness of his face and his eyes were
deep and dark. He looked at Shipstead and Wright and
he made no effort to hide the disgust in his voice.

"Your pigs are dead and buried."

As his gaze shifted to father, his face softened. But the
voice was still bitter. "There's another one down. Chris
won't be bothering anybody for quite a spell." He turned
and disappeared and we could hear him leading the horse
into the barn.

In the quiet following, hoofbeats like an echo sounded
in the distance. They swelled louder and this second horse
galloped into our lane and pulled to a stop. Ed Howells
jumped to the porch and hurried in.

"Where's Shane?"

"Out in the barn," father said.

"Did he tell you what happened?"

"Not much," father said mildly. "Something about bury-
ing pigs."

Ed Howells slumped into a chair. He seemed a bit dazed.
The words came out of him slowly at first as he tried to
make the others grasp just how he felt. "I never saw anything like it," he said, and he told about it.

He had been in Grafton's store buying a few things,
not caring about going into the saloon because Chris and
Red Marlin, another of Fletcher's cowboys, had hands in
the evening poker game, when he noticed how still the
place was. He went over to sneak a look and there was
Shane just moving to the bar, cool and easy as if the room
was empty and he the only one in it. Neither Chris nor
Red Marlin was saying a word, though you might have
thought this was a good chance for them to cut loose with

some of their raw sarcasm. One look at Shane was enough to tell why. He was cool and easy, right enough. But there was a curious kind of smooth flow to his movements that made you realize without being conscious of thinking about it that being quiet was a mighty sensible way to be at the moment.

"Two bottles of soda pop," he called to Will Atkey. He leaned his back to the bar and looked the poker game over with what seemed a friendly interest while Will fetched the bottles from the store. Not another person even twitched a muscle. They were all watching him and wondering what the play was. He took the two bottles and walked to the table and set them down, reaching over to put one in front of Chris.

"The last time I was in here you bought me a drink. Now it's my turn."

The words sort of lingered in the stillness. He got the impression, Ed Howells said, that Shane meant just what the words said. He wanted to buy Chris a drink. He wanted Chris to take that bottle and grin at him and drink with him.

You could have heard a bug crawl, I guess, while Chris carefully laid down the cards in his right hand and stretched it to the bottle. He lifted it in a sudden jerk and flung it across the table at Shane.

So fast Shane moved, Ed Howells said, that the bottle was still in the air when he had dodged, lunged forward, grabbed Chris by the shirtfront and hauled him right out of his chair and over the table. As Chris struggled to get his feet under him, Shane let go the shirt and slapped him, sharp and stinging, three times, the hand flicking back and forth so quick you could hardly see it, the slaps sounding like pistol shots.

Shane stepped back and Chris stood swaying a little and shaking his head to clear it. He was a game one and mad down to his boots. He plunged in, fists smashing, and Shane let him come, slipping inside the flailing arms and jolting a powerful blow low into his stomach. As Chris gasped and his head came down, Shane brought his right hand up, open, and with the heel of it caught Chris full on the mouth, snapping his head back and raking up over the nose and eyes.

The force of it knocked Chris off balance and he staggered badly. His lips were crushed. Blood was dripping over them from his battered nose. His eyes were red and watery and he was having trouble seeing with them. His face, Ed Howells said, and shook a little as he said it, looked like a horse had stomped it. But he drove in again, swinging wildly.

Shane ducked under, caught one of the flying wrists, twisted the arm to lock it and keep it from bending, and swung his shoulder into the armpit. He yanked hard on the wrist and Chris went up and over him. As the body hurtled over, Shane kept hold of the arm and wrenched it sideways and let the weight bear on it and you could hear the bone crack as Chris crashed to the floor.

A long sobbing sigh came from Chris and that died away and there was not a sound in the room. Shane never looked at the crumpled figure. He was straight and deadly and still. Every line of him was alive and eager. But he stood motionless. Only his eyes shifted to search the faces of the others at the table. They stopped on Red Marlin and Red seemed to dwindle lower in his chair.

"Perhaps," Shane said softly, and the very softness of his voice sent shivers through Ed Howells, "perhaps you have something to say about soda pop or pigs."

Red Marlin sat quiet like he was trying not even to breathe. Tiny drops of sweat appeared on his forehead. He was frightened, maybe for the first time in his life, and the others knew it and he knew they knew and he did not care. And none of them blamed him at all.

Then, as they watched, the fire in Shane smouldered down and out. He seemed to withdraw back within himself. He forgot them all and turned toward Chris unconscious on the floor, and a sort of sadness, Ed Howells said, crept over him and held him. He bent and scooped the sprawling figure up in his arms and carried it to one of the other tables. Gently he set it down, the legs falling limp over the edge. He crossed to the bar and took the rag Will used to wipe it and returned to the table and tenderly cleared the blood from the face. He felt carefully along the broken arm and nodded to himself at what he felt.

All this while no one said a word. Not a one of them would have interfered with that man for a year's top wages. He spoke and his voice rang across the room at Red Marlin. "You'd better tote him home and get that arm fixed. Take right good care of him. He has the makings of a good man." Then he forgot them all again and looked at Chris and went on speaking as if to that limp figure that could not hear him. "There's only one thing really wrong with you. You're young. That's the one thing time can always cure."

The thought hurt him and he strode to the swinging doors and through them into the night. That was what Ed Howells told. "The whole business," he finished, "didn't take five minutes. It was maybe thirty seconds from the time he grabbed holt of Chris till Chris was out cold on the floor. In my opinion that Shane is the most dangerous man I've ever seen. I'm glad he's working for Joe here and not for Fletcher."

Father leveled a triumphant look at Henry Shipstead. "So I've made a mistake, have I?"

Before anyone else could push in a word, mother was speaking. I was surprised, because she was upset and her voice was a little shrill. "I wouldn't be too sure about that, Joe Starrett. I think you've made a bad mistake."

"Marian, what's got into you?"

"Look what you've done just because you got him to stay on here and get mixed up in this trouble with Fletcher!"

Father was edging toward being peeved himself. "Women never do understand these things. Lookahere, Marian. Chris will be all right. He's young and he's healthy. Soon as that arm is mended, he'll be in as good shape as he ever was."

"Oh, Joe, can't you see what I'm talking about? I don't mean what you've done to Chris. I mean what you've done to Shane."

8

THIS TIME mother was right. Shane was changed. He tried to keep things as they had been with us and on the surface nothing was different. But he had lost the serenity that had seeped into him through the summer. He would no longer sit around and talk with us as much as he had. He was restless with some far hidden desperation.

At times, when it rode him worst, he would wander alone about our place, and this was the one thing that seemed to soothe him. I used to see him, when he thought no one was watching, run his hands along the rails of the corral he had fastened, test with a tug the posts he had set, pace out past the barn looking up at the bulging loft and stride out where the tall corn was standing in big shocks to dig his hands in the loose soil and lift some of it and let it run through his fingers.

He would lean on the pasture fence and study our little herd like it meant more to him than lazy steers to be fattened for market. Sometimes he would whistle softly, and his horse, filled out now so you could see the quality of him and moving with a quiet sureness and power that made you think of Shane himself, would trot to the fence and nuzzle at him.

Often he would disappear from the house in the early evening after supper. More than once, the dishes done, when I managed to slip past mother, I found him far back in the pasture alone with the horse. He would be standing there, one arm on the smooth arch of the horse's neck, the fingers gently rubbing around the ears, and he would be looking out over our land where the last light of the sun, now out of sight, would be flaring up the far side of the mountains, capping them with a deep glow and leaving a mystic gloaming in the valley.

Some of the assurance that was in him when he came was gone now. He seemed to feel that he needed to justify himself, even to me, to a boy tagging his heels.

"Could you teach me," I asked him, "to throw somebody the way you threw Chris?"

He waited so long I thought he would not answer. "A man doesn't learn things like that," he said at last. "You know them and that's all." Then he was talking rapidly to me, as close to pleading as he could ever come. "I tried. You can see that, can't you, Bob? I let him ride me and I gave him his chance. A man can keep his self-respect without having to cram it down another man's throat. Surely you can see that, Bob?"

I could not see it. What he was trying to explain to me was beyond my comprehension then. And I could think of nothing to say.

"I left it up to him. He didn't have to jump me that second time. He could have called it off without crawling. He could have if he was man enough. Can't you see that, Bob?"

And still I could not. But I said I could. He was so earnest and he wanted me to so badly. It was a long, long time before I did see it and then I was a man myself and Shane was not there for me to tell. . . .

I was not sure whether father and mother were aware of the change in him. They did not talk about it, not while I was around anyway. But one afternoon I overheard something that showed mother knew.

I had hurried home from school and put on my old clothes and started out to see what father and Shane were doing in the cornfield, when I thought of a trick that had worked several times. Mother was firm set against eating between meals. That was a silly notion. I had my mind set on the cookies she kept in a tin box on a shelf by the stove. She was settled on the porch with a batch of potatoes to peel, so I slipped up to the back of the house, through the window of my little room, and tiptoed into the kitchen. Just as I was carefully putting a chair under the shelf, I heard her call to Shane.

He must have come to the barn on some errand, for he was there by the porch in only a moment. I peered out the front window and saw him standing close in, his hat in his hand, his face tilted up slightly to look at her leaning forward in her chair.

"I've been wanting to talk to you when Joe wasn't around."

"Yes, Marian." He called her that the same as father did, familiar yet respectful, just as he always regarded her with a tenderness in his eyes he had for no one else.

"You've been worrying, haven't you, about what may happen in this Fletcher business? You thought it would just be a case of not letting him scare you away and of helping us through a hard time. You didn't know it would come to what it has. And now you're worried about what you might do if there's any more fighting."

"You're a discerning woman, Marian."

"You've been worrying about something else too."

"You're a mighty discerning woman, Marian."

"And you've been thinking that maybe you'll be moving on."

"And how did you know that?"

"Because it's what you ought to do. For your own sake. But I'm asking you not to." Mother was intense and serious, as lovely there with the light striking through her hair as I had ever seen her. "Don't go, Shane. Joe needs you. More than ever now. More than he would ever say."

"And you?" Shane's lips barely moved and I was not sure of the words.

Mother hesitated. Then her head went up. "Yes. It's only fair to say it. I need you too."

"So-o-o," he said softly, the words lingering on his lips. He considered her gravely. "Do you know what you're asking, Marian?"

"I know. And I know that you're the man to stand up to it. In some ways it would be easier for me, too, if you rode out of this valley and never came back. But we can't let Joe down. I'm counting on you not ever to make me do that. Because you've got to stay, Shane, no matter how hard it is for us. Joe can't keep this place without you. He can't buck Fletcher alone."

Shane was silent, and it seemed to me that he was troubled and hard pressed in his mind. Mother was talking straight to him, slow and feeling for the words, and her voice was beginning to tremble.

"It would just about kill Joe to lose this place. He's too old to start in again somewhere else. Oh, we would get along and might even do real well. After all, he's Joe Starrett. He's all man and he can do what has to be done. But he promised me this place when we were married. He had it in his mind for all the first years. He did two men's work to get the extra money for the things we would need. When Bob was big enough to walk and help some and he could leave us, he came on here and filed his claim and built this house with his own hands, and when he brought us here it was home. Nothing else would ever be the same."

Shane drew a deep breath and let it ease out slowly. He smiled at her and yet, somehow, as I watched him, my heart ached for him. "Joe should be proud of a wife like you. Don't fret any more, Marian. You'll not lose this place."

Mother dropped back in her chair. Her face, the side I could see from the window, was radiant. Then, woman like, she was talking against herself. "But that Fletcher is a mean and tricky man. Are you sure it will work out all right?"

Shane was already starting toward the barn. He stopped and turned to look at her again. "I said you won't lose this place." You knew he was right because of the way he said it and because he said it.

9

A NOTHER PERIOD of peace had settled over our valley. Since the night Shane rode into town, Fletcher's cowboys had quit using the road past the homesteads. They were not annoying us at all and only once in a while was there a rider in view across the river. They had a good excuse to let us be. They were busy fixing the ranch buildings and poling a big new corral in preparation for the spring drive of new cattle Fletcher was planning.

Just the same, I noticed that father was as watchful as Shane now. The two of them worked always together. They did not split any more to do separate jobs in different parts of the farm. They worked together, rode into town together when anything was needed. And father took to wearing his gun all the time, even in the fields. He strapped it on after breakfast the first morning following the fight with Chris, and I saw him catch Shane's eye with a questioning glance as he buckled the belt. But Shane shook his head and father nodded, accepting the decision, and they went out together without saying a word.

Those were beautiful fall days, clear and stirring, with the coolness in the air just enough to set one atingling, not yet mounting to the bitter cold that soon would come sweeping down out of the mountains. It did not seem possible that in such a harvest season, giving a lift to the spirit to match the wellbeing of the body, violence could flare so suddenly and swiftly.

Saturday evenings all of us would pile into the light work wagon, father and mother on the seat, Shane and I swinging legs at the rear, and go into town. It was the break in routine we looked forward to all week.

There was always a bustle in Grafton's store with people we knew coming and going. Mother would lay in her supplies for the week ahead, taking a long time about it and chatting with the womenfolk. She and the wives of the other homesteaders were great ones for swapping recipes and this was their bartering ground. Father would give Mr. Grafton his order for what he wanted and go direct for the mail. He was always getting catalogues of farm equipment and pamphlets from Washington. He would flip through their pages and skim through any letters, then settle on a barrel and spread out his newspaper. But like as not he would soon be bogged down in an argument with almost any man handy about the best crops for the Territory and it would be Shane who would really work his way into the newspaper.

I used to explore the store, filling myself with crackers from the open barrel at the end of the main counter, playing hide and seek with Mr. Grafton's big and knowing old cat that was a whiz of a mouser. Many a time, turning up boxes, I chased out fat furry ones for her to pounce on. If mother was in the right mood, I would have a bag of candy in my pocket.

This time we had a special reason for staying longer than usual, a reason I did not like. Our schoolteacher, Jane Grafton, had made me take a note home to mother asking her to stop in for a talk. About me. I never was too smart at formal schooling to begin with. Being all excited over the doings at the big ranch and what they might mean to us had not helped any. Miss Grafton, I guess, just sort of endured me under the best of conditions. But what tipped her into being downright annoyed and writing to mother was the weather. No one could expect a boy with any spirit in him to be shut up in a schoolroom in weather like we had been having. Twice that week I had persuaded Ollie Johnson to sneak away with me after the lunch hour to see if the fish were still biting in our favorite pool below town.

Mother finished the last item on her list, looked around at me, sighed a little, and stiffened her shoulders. I knew she was going to the living quarters behind the store and talk to Miss Grafton. I squirmed and pretended I did not notice her. Only a few people were left in the store, though the saloon in the adjoining big room was doing fair business. She went over to where father was leafing through a catalogue and tapped him.

"Come along, Joe. You should hear this, too. I declare, that boy is getting too big for me to handle."

Father glanced quickly over the store and paused, listening to the voices from the next room. We had not seen any of Fletcher's men all evening and he seemed satisfied. He looked at Shane, who was folding the newspaper.

"This won't take long. We'll be out in a moment."

As they passed through the door at the rear of the store, Shane strolled to the saloon opening. He took in the whole room in his easy, alert way and stepped inside. I followed. But I was supposed not ever to go in there, so I stopped at the entrance. Shane was at the bar, joshing Will Atkey with a grave face that he didn't think he'd have soda pop tonight. It was a scattered group in the room, most of them from around town and familiar to me by sight at least. Those close to Shane moved a little away, eyeing him curiously. He did not appear to notice.

He picked up his drink and savored it, one elbow on the bar, not shoving himself forward into the room's companionship and not withdrawing either, just ready to be friendly if anyone wanted that and unfriendly if anyone wanted that too.

I was letting my eyes wander about, trying to tag names to faces, when I saw that one of the swinging doors was partly open and Red Marlin was peeking in. Shane saw it too. But he could not see that more men were out on the porch, for they were close by the building wall and on the store side. I could sense them through the window near me, hulking shapes in the darkness. I was so frightened I could scarcely move.

But I had to. I had to go against mother's rule. I scrambled into the saloon and to Shane and I gasped: "Shane! There's a lot of them out front!"

I was too late. Red Marlin was inside and the others were hurrying in and fanning out to close off the store opening. Morgan was one of them, his flat face sour and determined, his huge shoulders almost filling the doorway as he came through. Behind him was the cowboy they called Curly because of his shock of unruly hair. He was stupid and slow-moving, but he was thick and powerful, and he had worked in harness with Chris for several years. Two others followed them, new men to me, with the tough, experienced look of old herd hands.

There was still the back office with its outside door opening on a side stoop and the rear alley. My knees were shaking and I tugged at Shane and tried to say something about it. He stopped me with a sharp gesture. His face was clear, his eyes bright. He was somehow happy, not in the pleased and laughing way, but happy that the waiting was over and what had been ahead was here and seen and realized and he was ready for it. He put one hand on my head and rocked it gently, the fingers feeling through my hair.

"Bobby boy, would you have me run away?"

Love for that man raced through me and the warmth ran down and stiffened my legs and I was so proud of being there with him that I could not keep the tears from my eyes. I could see the rightness of it and I was ready to do as he told me when he said: "Get out of here, Bob. This isn't going to be pretty."

But I would go no farther than my perch just inside the store where I could watch most of the big room. I was so bound in the moment that I did not even think of running for father.

Morgan was in the lead now with his men spread out behind him. He came about half the way to Shane and stopped. The room was quiet except for the shuffling of feet as the men by the bar and the nearest tables hastened over to the far wall and some of them ducked out the front doors. Neither Shane nor Morgan gave any attention to them. They had attention only for each other. They did not look aside even when Mr. Grafton, who could smell trouble in his place from any distance, stalked in from the store, planting his feet down firmly, and pushed past

Will Atkey behind the bar. He had a resigned expression on his face and he reached under the counter, his hands reappearing with a short-barreled shotgun. He laid it before him on the bar and he said in a dry, disgusted voice: "There will be no gunplay, gentlemen. And all damages will be paid for."

Morgan nodded curtly, not taking his eyes from Shane. He came closer and stopped again little more than an arm's length away. His head was thrust forward. His big fists were clenched at his sides.

"No one messes up one of my boys and gets away with it. We're riding you out of this valley on a rail, Shane. We're going to rough you a bit and ride you out and you'll stay out."

"So you have it all planned," Shane said softly. Even as he was speaking, he was moving. He flowed into action so swift you could hardly believe what was happening. He scooped up his half-filled glass from the bar, whipped it and its contents into Morgan's face, and when Morgan's hands came up reaching or striking for him, he grasped the wrists and flung himself backwards, dragging Morgan with him. His body rolled to meet the floor and his legs doubled and his feet, catching Morgan just below the belt, sent him flying on and over to fall flat in a grotesque spraddle and slide along the boards in a tangle of chairs and a table.

The other four were on Shane in a rush. As they came, he whirled to his hands and knees and leaped up and behind the nearest table, tipping it in a strong heave among them. They scattered, dodging, and he stepped, fast and light, around the end and drove into the tail man, one of the new men, now nearest to him. He took the blows at him straight on to get in close and I saw his knee surge up and into the man's groin. A high scream was literally torn from the man and he collapsed to the floor and dragged himself toward the doors.

Morgan was on his feet, wavering, rubbing a hand across his face, staring hard as if trying to focus again on the room about him. The other three were battering at Shane, seeking to box him between them. They were piling blows into him, crowding in. Through that blur of movement he was weaving, quick and confident. It was incredible, but they could not hurt him. You could see the blows hit, hear the solid chunk of knuckles on flesh. But they had no effect. They seemed only to feed that fierce energy. He moved like a flame among them. He would burst out of the mêlée and whirl and plunge back, the one man actually pressing the three. He had picked the second new man and was driving always directly at him.

Curly, slow and clumsy, grunting in exasperation, grabbed at Shane to grapple with him and hold down his arms. Shane dropped one shoulder and as Curly hugged tighter brought it up under his jaw with a jolt that knocked him loose and away.

They were wary now and none too eager to let him get close to any one of them. Then Red Marlin came at him from one side, forcing him to turn that way, and at the same time the second new man did a strange thing. He jumped high in the air, like a jack rabbit in a spy hop, and lashed out viciously with one boot at Shane's head. Shane saw it coming, but could not avoid it, so he rolled his head with the kick, taking it along the side. It shook him badly. But it did not block the instant response. His hands shot up and seized the foot and the man crashed down to land on the small of his back. As he hit, Shane twisted the whole leg and threw his weight on it. The man buckled on the floor like a snake when you hit it and groaned sharply and hitched himself away, the leg dragging, the fight gone out of him.

But the swing to bend down on the leg had put Shane's back to Curly and the big man was plowing at him. Curly's arms clamped around him, pinning his arms to his body. Red Marlin leaped to help and the two of them had Shane caught tight between them.

"Hold him!" That was Morgan, coming forward with the hate plain in his eyes. Even then, Shane would have broke away. He stomped one heavy work shoe, heel edged and with all the strength he could get in quick leverage, on Curly's near foot. As Curly winced and pulled it back and was unsteady, Shane strained with his whole body in a powerful arch and you could see their arms slipping and loosening. Morgan, circling in, saw it too. He swept a bottle off the bar and brought it smashing down from behind on Shane's head.

Shane slumped and would have fallen if they had not been holding him. Then, as Morgan stepped around in front of him and watched, the vitality pumped through him and his head came up.

"Hold him!" Morgan said again. He deliberately flung a huge fist to Shane's face. Shane tried to jerk aside and the fist missed the jaw, tearing along the cheek, the heavy ring on one finger slicing deep. Morgan pulled back for another blow. He never made it.

Nothing, I would have said, could have drawn my attention from those men. But I heard a kind of choking sob beside me and it was queer and yet familiar and it turned me instantly.

Father was there in the entranceway!

He was big and terrible and he was looking across the overturned table and scattered chairs at Shane, at the dark purplish bruise along the side of Shane's head and the blood running down his cheek. I had never seen father like this. He was past anger. He was filled with a fury that was shaking him almost beyond endurance.

I never thought he could move so fast. He was on them before they even knew he was in the room. He hurtled into Morgan with ruthless force, sending that huge man reeling across the room. He reached out one broad hand and grabbed Curly by the shoulder and you could see the fingers sink into the flesh. He took hold of Curly's belt with the other hand and ripped him loose from Shane and his own shirt shredded down the back and the great muscles there knotted and bulged as he lifted Curly right up over his head and hurled the threshing body from him. Curly spun through the air, his limbs waving wildly, and crashed on the top of a table way over by the wall. It cracked under him, collapsing in splintered pieces, and the man and the wreckage smacked against the wall. Curly tried to rise, pushing himself with hands on the floor, and fell back and was still.

Shane must have exploded into action the second father yanked Curly away, for now there was another noise. It was Red Marlin, his face contorted, flung against the bar and catching at it to keep himself from falling. He staggered and caught his balance and ran for the front doorway. His flight was frantic, headlong. He tore through the swinging doors without slowing to push them. They flapped with a swishing sound and my eyes shifted quickly to Shane, for he was laughing.

He was standing there, straight and superb, the blood on his face bright like a badge, and he was laughing.

It was a soft laugh, soft and gentle, not in amusement at Red Marlin or any single thing, but in the joy of being alive and released from long discipline and answering the urge in mind and body. The lithe power in him, so different from father's sheer strength, was singing in every fiber of him.

Morgan was in the rear corner, his face clouded and uncertain. Father, his fury eased by the mighty effort of throwing Curly, had looked around to watch Red Marlin's run and now was starting toward Morgan. Shane's voice stopped him.

"Wait, Joe. The man's mine." He was at father's side and he put a hand on father's arm. "You'd better get them out of here." He nodded in my direction and I noticed with surprise that mother was near and watching. She must have followed father and have been there all this while. Her lips were parted. Her eyes were glowing, looking at the whole room, not at anyone or anything in particular, but at the whole room.

Father was disappointed. "Morgan's more my size," he said, grumbling fashion. He was not worried about Shane. He was thinking of an excuse to take Morgan himself. But he went no further. He looked at the men over by the wall. "This is Shane's play. If a one of you tries to interfere, he'll have me to reckon with." His tone showed that he was not mad at them, that he was not even really

warning them. He was simply making the play plain. Then
he came to us and looked down at mother. "You wait out
at the wagon, Marian. Morgan's had this coming to him for
quite a long time now and it's not for a woman to see."

Mother shook her head without moving her eyes now
from Shane. "No, Joe. He's one of us. I'll see this through."
And the three of us stayed there together and that was
right, for he was Shane.

He advanced toward Morgan, as flowing and graceful
as the old mouser in the store. He had forgotten us and
the battered men on the floor and those withdrawn by the
wall and Mr. Grafton and Will Atkey crouched behind
the bar. His whole being was concentrated on the big man
before him.

Morgan was taller, half again as broad, with a long
reputation as a bullying fighter in the valley. But he did
not like this and he was desperate. He knew better than
to wait. He rushed at Shane to overwhelm the smaller
man with his weight. Shane faded from in front of him
and as Morgan went past hooked a sharp blow to his
stomach and another to the side of his jaw. They were
short and quick, flicking in so fast they were just a blur
of movement. Yet each time at the instant of impact
Morgan's big frame shook and halted in its rush for a
fraction of a second before the momentum carried him
forward. Again and again he rushed, driving his big fists
ahead. Always Shane slipped away, sending in those swift
hard punches.

Breathing heavily, Morgan stopped, grasping the futility
of straight fighting. He plunged at Shane now, arms wide,
trying to get hold of him and wrestle him down. Shane
was ready and let him come without dodging, disregarding
the arms stretching to encircle him. He brought up his
right hand, open, just as Ed Howells had told us, and the
force of Morgan's own lunge as the hand met his mouth
and raked upwards snapped back his head and sent him
staggering.

Morgan's face was puffy and red-mottled. He bellowed
some insane sound and swung up a chair. Holding it in

front of him, legs forward, he rushed again at Shane, who sidestepped neatly. Morgan was expecting this and halted suddenly, swinging the chair in a swift arc to strike Shane with it full on the side. The chair shattered and Shane faltered, and then, queerly for a man usually so sure on his feet, he seemed to slip and fall to the floor.

Forgetting all caution, Morgan dove at him—and Shane's legs bent and he caught Morgan on his heavy work shoes and sent him flying back and against the bar with a crash that shook the whole length of it.

Shane was up and leaping at Morgan as if there had been springs under him there on the floor. His left hand, palm out, smacked against Morgan's forehead, pushing the head back, and his right fist drove straight to Morgan's throat. You could see the agony twist the man's face and the fear widen his eyes. And Shane, using his right fist now like a club and lining his whole body behind it, struck him on the neck below and back of the ear. It made a sickening, dull sound and Morgan's eyes rolled white and he went limp all over, sagging slowly and forward to the floor.

10

IN THE HUSH that followed Morgan's fall, the big barroom was so quiet again that the rustle of Will Atkey straightening from below the bar level was loud and clear and Will stopped moving, embarrassed and a little frightened.

Shane looked neither at him nor at any of the other men staring from the wall. He looked only at us, at father and mother and me, and it seemed to me that it hurt him to see us there.

He breathed deeply and his chest filled and he held it,

held it long and achingly, and released it slowly and sighing. Suddenly you were impressed by the fact that he was quiet, that he was still. You saw how battered and bloody he was. In the moments before you saw only the splendor of movement, the flowing brute beauty of line and power in action. The man, you felt, was tireless and indestructible. Now that he was still and the fire in him banked and subsided, you saw, and in the seeing remembered, that he had taken bitter punishment.

His shirt collar was dark and sodden. Blood was soaking into it, and this came only in part from the cut on his cheek. More was oozing from the matted hair where Morgan's bottle had hit. Unconsciously he put up one hand and it came away smeared and sticky. He regarded it grimly and wiped it clean on his shirt. He swayed slightly and when he started toward us, his feet dragged and he almost fell forward.

One of the townsmen, Mr. Weir, a friendly man who kept the stage post, pushed out from the wall, clucking sympathy, as though to help him. Shane pulled himself erect. His eyes blazed refusal. Straight and superb, not a tremor in him, he came to us and you knew that the spirit in him would sustain him thus alone for the farthest distance and forever.

But there was no need. The one man in our valley, the one man, I believe, in all the world whose help he would take, not to whom he would turn but whose help he would take, was there and ready. Father stepped to meet him and put out a big arm reaching for his shoulders. "All right, Joe," Shane said, so softly I doubt whether the others in the room heard. His eyes closed and he leaned against father's arm, his body relaxing and his head dropping sideways. Father bent and fitted his other arm under Shane's knees and picked him up like he did me when I stayed up too late and got all drowsy and had to be carried to bed.

Father held Shane in his arms and looked over him at Mr. Grafton. "I'd consider it a favor, Sam, if you'd figure the damage and put it on my bill."

For a man strict about bills and keen for a bargain, Mr.

Grafton surprised me. "I'm marking this to Fletcher's account. I'm seeing that he pays."

Mr. Weir surprised me even more. He spoke promptly and he was emphatic about it. "Listen to me, Starrett. It's about time this town worked up a little pride. Maybe it's time, too, we got to be more neighborly with you homesteaders. I'll take a collection to cover this. I've been ashamed of myself ever since it started tonight, standing here and letting five of them jump that man of yours."

Father was pleased. But he knew what he wanted to do. "That's mighty nice of you, Weir. But this ain't your fight. I wouldn't worry, was I you, about keeping out of it." He looked down at Shane and the pride was plain busting out of him. "Matter of fact, I'd say the odds tonight, without me butting in, too, was mighty close to even." He looked again at Mr. Grafton. "Fletcher ain't getting in on this with a nickel. I'm paying." He tossed back his head. "No, by Godfrey! We're paying. Me and Shane."

He went to the swinging doors, turning sideways to push them open. Mother took my hand and we followed. She always knew when to talk and when not to talk, and she said no word while we watched father lift Shane to the wagon seat, climb beside him, hoist him to sitting position with one arm around him and take the reins in the other hand. Will Atkey trotted out with our things and stowed them away. Mother and I perched on the back of the wagon, father chirruped to the team, and we were started home.

There was not a sound for quite a stretch except the clop of hooves and the little creakings of the wheels. Then I heard a chuckle up front. It was Shane. The cool air was reviving him and he was sitting straight, swaying with the wagon's motion.

"What did you do with the thick one, Joe? I was busy with the redhead."

"Oh, I just kind of tucked him out of the way." Father wanted to let it go at that. Not mother.

"He picked him up like—like a bag of potatoes and

threw him clear across the room." She did not say it to Shane, not to any person. She said it to the night, to the sweet darkness around us, and her eyes were shining in the starlight.

We turned in at our place and father shooed the rest of us into the house while he unhitched the team. In the kitchen mother set some water to heat on the stove and chased me to bed. Her back was barely to me after she tucked me in before I was peering around the door jamb. She got several clean rags, took the water from the stove, and went to work on Shane's head. She was tender as could be, crooning like to herself under her breath the while. It pained him plenty as the warm water soaked into the gash under the matted hair and as she washed the clotted blood from his cheek. But it seemed to pain her more, for her hand shook at the worst moments, and she was the one who flinched while he sat there quietly and smiled reassuringly at her.

Father came in and sat by the stove, watching them. He pulled out his pipe and made a very careful business of packing it and lighting it.

She finished. Shane would not let her try a bandage. "This air is the best medicine," he said. She had to be content with cleaning the cuts thoroughly and making certain all bleeding had stopped. Then it was father's turn.

"Get that shirt off, Joe. It's torn all down the back. Let me see what I can do with it." Before he could rise, she had changed her mind. "No. We'll keep it just like it is. To remember tonight by. You were magnificent, Joe, tearing that man away and—"

"Shucks," said father. "I was just peeved. Him holding Shane so Morgan could pound him."

"And you, Shane." Mother was in the middle of the kitchen, looking from one to the other. "You were magnificent, too. Morgan was so big and horrible and yet he didn't have even a chance. You were so cool and quick and—and dangerous and—"

"A woman shouldn't have to see things like that." Shane interrupted her, and he meant it. But she was talking right ahead.

"You think I shouldn't because it's brutal and nasty and not just fighting to see who is better at it, but mean and vicious and to win by any way, but to win. Of course it is. But you didn't start it. You didn't want to do it. Not until they made you anyway. You did it because you had to."

Her voice was climbing and she was looking back and forth and losing control of herself. "Did ever a woman have two such men?" And she turned from them and reached out blindly for a chair and sank into it and dropped her face into her hands and the tears came.

The two men stared at her and then at each other in that adult knowledge beyond my understanding. Shane rose and stepped over by mother. He put a hand gently on her head and I felt again his fingers in my hair and the affection flooding through me. He walked quietly out the door and into the night.

Father drew on his pipe. It was out and absently he lit it. He rose and went to the door and out on the porch. I could see him there dimly in the darkness, gazing across the river.

Gradually mother's sobs died down. She raised her head and wiped away the tears.

"Joe."

He turned and started in and waited then by the door. She stood up. She stretched her hands toward him and he was there and had her in his arms.

"Do you think I don't know, Marian?"

"But you don't. Not really. You can't. Because I don't know myself."

Father was staring over her head at the kitchen wall, not seeing anything there. "Don't fret yourself, Marian. I'm man enough to know a better when his trail meets mine. Whatever happens will be all right."

"Oh, Joe . . . Joe! Kiss me. Hold me tight and don't ever let go."

11

WHAT HAPPENED in our kitchen that night was beyond me in those days. But it did not worry me because father had said it would be all right, and how could anyone, knowing him, doubt that he would make it so.

And we were not bothered by Fletcher's men any more at all. There might not have been a big ranch on the other side of the river, sprawling up the valley and over on our side above Ernie Wright's place, for all you could tell from our house. They left us strictly alone and were hardly ever seen now even in town. Fletcher himself, I heard from kids at school, was gone again. He went on the stage to Cheyenne and maybe farther, and nobody seemed to know why he went.

Yet father and Shane were more wary than they had been before. They stayed even closer together and they spent no more time than they had to in the fields. There was no more talking on the porch in the evenings, though the nights were so cool and lovely they called you to be out and under the winking stars. We kept to the house, and father insisted on having the lamps well shaded and he polished his rifle and hung it, ready loaded, on a couple of nails by the kitchen door.

All this caution failed to make sense to me. So at dinner about a week later I asked: "Is there something new that's wrong? That stuff about Fletcher is finished, isn't it?"

"Finished?" said Shane, looking at me over his coffee cup. "Bobby boy, it's only begun."

"That's right," said father. "Fletcher's gone too far to back out now. It's a case of now or never with him. If he can make us run, he'll be setting pretty for a long stretch. If he can't, it'll be only a matter o' time before he's shoved smack out of this valley. There's three or four of the men who looked through here last year ready right now to sharpen stakes and move in soon as they think it's safe. I'll bet Fletcher feels he got aholt of a bear by the tail and it'd be nice to be able to let go."

"Why doesn't he do something, then?" I asked. "Seems to me mighty quiet around here lately."

"Seems to you, eh?" said father. "Seems to me you're mighty young to be doing much seemsing. Don't you worry, son. Fletcher is fixing to do something. The grass that grows under his feet won't feed any cow. I'd be easier in my mind if I knew what he's up to."

"You see, Bob"—Shane was speaking to me the way I liked, as if maybe I was a man and could understand all he said—"by talking big and playing it rough, Fletcher has made this a straight win or lose deal. It's the same as if he'd kicked loose a stone that starts a rockslide and all he can do is hope to ride it down and hit bottom safe. Maybe he doesn't realize that yet. I think he does. And don't let things being quiet fool you. When there's noise, you know where to look and what's happening. When things are quiet, you've got to be most careful."

Mother sighed. She was looking at Shane's cheek where the cut was healing into a scar like a thin line running back from near the mouth corner. "I suppose you two are right. But does there have to be any more fighting?"

"Like the other night?" asked father. "No, Marian, I don't think so. Fletcher knows better now."

"He knows better," Shane said, "because he knows it won't work. If he's the man I think he is, he's known that since the first time he sicced Chris on me. I doubt that was his move the other night. That was Morgan's. Fletcher'll be watching for some way that has more finesse —and will be more final."

"Hm-m-m," said father, a little surprised. "Some legal trick, eh?"

"Could be. If he can find one. If not—" Shane shrugged and gazed out the window. "There are other ways. You can't call a man like Fletcher on things like that. Depends on how far he's willing to go. But whatever he does, once he's ready, he'll do it speedy and sure."

"Hm-m-m," said father again. "Now you put it that-away, I see you're right. That's Fletcher's way. Bet you've bumped against someone like him before." When Shane did not answer, just kept staring out the window, he went on. "Wish I could be as patient about it as you. I don't like this waiting."

But we did not have to wait long. It was the next day, a Friday, when we were finishing supper, that Lew Johnson and Henry Shipstead brought us the news. Fletcher was back and he had not come back alone. There was another man with him.

Lew Johnson saw them as they got off the stage. He had a good chance to look the stranger over while they waited in front of the post for horses to be brought in from the ranch. Since it was beginning to get dark, he had not been able to make out the stranger's face too well. The light striking through the post window, however, was enough for him to see what kind of man he was.

He was tall, rather broad in the shoulders and slim in the waist. He carried himself with a sort of swagger. He had a mustache that he favored and his eyes, when Johnson saw them reflecting the light from the window, were cold and had a glitter that bothered Johnson.

This stranger was something of a dude about his clothes. Still, that did not mean anything. When he turned, the coat he wore matching his pants flapped open and Johnson could see what had been half-hidden before. He was carrying two guns, big capable forty-fives, in holsters hung fairly low and forward. Those holsters were pegged down at the tips with thin straps fastened around the man's legs. Johnson said he saw the tiny buckles when the light flashed on them.

Wilson was the man's name. That was what Fletcher called him when a cowboy rode up leading a couple of horses. A funny other name. Stark. Stark Wilson. And that was not all.

Lew Johnson was worried and went into Grafton's to find Will Atkey, who always knew more than anyone else about people apt to be coming along the road because he was constantly picking up information from the talk of men drifting in to the bar. Will would not believe it at first when Johnson told him the name. What would he be doing up here, Will kept saying. Then Will blurted out that this Wilson was a bad one, a killer. He was a gun-fighter said to be just as good with either hand and as fast on the draw as the best of them. He came to Cheyenne from Kansas, Will claimed he had heard, with a reputation for killing three men there and nobody knew how many more down in the southwest territories where he used to be.

Lew Johnson was rattling on, adding details as he could think of them. Henry Shipstead was slumped in a chair by the stove. Father was frowning at his pipe, absently fishing in a pocket for a match. It was Shane who shut off Johnson with a suddenness that startled the rest of us. His voice was sharp and clear and it seemed to crackle in the air. You could feel him taking charge of that room and all of us in it.

"When did they hit town?"

"Last night."

"And you waited till now to tell it!" There was disgust in Shane's voice. "You're a farmer all right, Johnson. That's all you ever will be." He whirled on father. "Quick, Joe. Which one has the hottest head? Which one's the easiest to prod into being a fool? Torrey is it? Or Wright?"

"Ernie Wright," father said slowly.

"Get moving, Johnson. Get out there on your horse and make it to Wright's in a hurry. Bring him here. Pick up Torrey, too. But get Wright first."

"He'll have to go into town for that," Henry Shipstead said heavily. "We passed them both down the road riding in."

Shane jumped to his feet. Lew Johnson was shuffling reluctantly toward the door. Shane brushed him aside. He strode to the door himself, yanked it open, started out. He stopped, leaning forward and listening.

"Hell, man," Henry Shipstead was grumbling, "what's your hurry? We told them about Wilson. They'll stop here on their way back." His voice ceased. All of us could hear it now, a horse pounding up the road at full gallop.

Shane turned back into the room. "There's your answer," he said bitterly. He swung the nearest chair to the wall and sat down. The fire blazing in him a moment before was gone. He was withdrawn into his own thoughts, and they were dark and not pleasant.

We heard the horse sliding to a stop out front. The sound was so plain you could fairly see the forelegs bracing and the hooves digging into the ground. Frank Torrey burst into the doorway. His hat was gone, his hair blowing wild. His chest heaved like he had been running as hard as the horse. He put his hands on the doorposts to hold himself steady and his voice was a hoarse whisper, though he was trying to shout across the room at father.

"Ernie's shot! They've killed him!"

The words jerked us to our feet and we stood staring. All but Shane. He did not move. You might have thought he was not even interested in what Torrey had said.

Father was the one who took hold of the scene. "Come in, Frank," he said quietly. "I take it we're too late to help Ernie now. Sit down and talk and don't leave anything out." He led Frank Torrey to a chair and pushed him into it. He closed the door and returned to his own chair. He looked older and tired.

It took Frank Torrey quite a while to pull himself together and tell his story straight. He was frightened. The fear was bedded deep in him and he was ashamed of himself for it.

He and Ernie Wright, he told us, had been to the stage office asking for a parcel Ernie was expecting. They dropped into Grafton's for a freshener before starting back. Since things had been so quiet lately, they were not thinking of any trouble even though Fletcher and the new man, Stark Wilson, were in the poker game at the big table. But Fletcher and Wilson must have been watching for a chance like that. They chucked in their hands and came over to the bar.

Fletcher was nice and polite as could be, nodding to Torrey and singling out Ernie for talk. He said he was sorry about it, but he really needed the land Ernie had filed on. It was the right place to put up winter wind-shelters for the new herd he was bringing in soon. He knew Ernie had not proved up on it yet. Just the same, he was willing to pay a fair price.

"I'll give you three hundred dollars," he said, "and that's more than the lumber in your buildings will be worth to me."

Ernie had more than that of his money in the place already. He had turned Fletcher down three or four times before. He was mad, the way he always was when Fletcher started his smooth talk.

"No," he said shortly. "I'm not selling. Not now or ever."

Fletcher shrugged like he had done all he could and slipped a quick nod at Stark Wilson. This Wilson was half-smiling at Ernie. But his eyes, Frank Torrey said, had nothing like a smile in them.

"I'd change my mind if I were you," he said to Ernie. "That is, if you have a mind to change."

"Keep out of this," snapped Ernie. "It's none of your business."

"I see you haven't heard," Wilson said softly. "I'm Mr. Fletcher's new business agent. I'm handling his business affairs for him. His business with stubborn jackasses like you." Then he said what showed Fletcher had coaxed him to it. "You're a damn fool, Wright. But what can you expect from a breed?"

"That's a lie!" shouted Ernie. "My mother wasn't no Indian!"

"Why, you crossbred squatter," Wilson said, quick and sharp, "are you telling me I'm wrong?"

"I'm telling you you're a God-damned liar!"

The silence that shut down over the saloon was so complete, Frank Torrey told us, that he could hear the ticking of the old alarm clock on the shelf behind the bar. Even Ernie, in the second his voice stopped, saw what he had done. But he was mad clear through and he glared at Wilson, his eyes reckless.

"So-o-o-o," said Wilson, satisfied now and stretching out the word with ominous softness. He flipped back his coat on the right side in front and the holster there was free with the gun grip ready for his hand.

"You'll back that, Wright. Or you'll crawl out of here on your belly."

Ernie moved out a step from the bar, his arms stiff at his sides. The anger in him held him erect as he beat down the terror tearing at him. He knew what this meant, but he met it straight. His hand was firm on his gun and pulling up when Wilson's first bullet hit him and staggered him. The second spun him halfway around and a faint froth appeared on his lips and all expression died from his face and he sagged to the floor.

While Frank Torrey was talking, Jim Lewis and a few minutes later Ed Howells had come in. Bad news travels fast and they seemed to know something was wrong. Perhaps they had heard that frantic galloping, the sound carrying far in the still night air. They were all in our kitchen now and they were more shaken and sober than I had ever seen them.

I was pressed close to mother, grateful for her arms around me. I noticed that she had little attention for the other men. She was watching Shane, bitter and silent across the room.

"So that's it," father said grimly. "We'll have to face it. We sell and at his price or he slips the leash on his hired killer. Did Wilson make a move toward you, Frank?"

"He looked at me." Simply recalling that made Torrey shiver through. "He looked at me and he said, 'Too bad, isn't it, mister, that Wright didn't change his mind?'"

"Then what?"

"I got out of there quick as I could and came here."

Jim Lewis had been fidgeting on his seat, more nervous

every minute. Now he jumped up, almost shouting. "But damn it, Joe! A man can't just go around shooting people!"

"Shut up, Jim," growled Henry Shipstead. "Don't you see the setup? Wilson badgered Ernie into getting himself in a spot where he had to go for his gun. Wilson can claim he shot in self-defense. He'll try the same thing on each of us."

"That's right, Jim," put in Lew Johnson. "Even if we tried to get a marshal in here, he couldn't hold Wilson. It was an even break and the faster man won is the way most people will figure it and plenty of them saw it. A marshal couldn't get here in time anyway."

"But we've got to stop it!" Lewis was really shouting now. "What chance have any of us got against Wilson? We're not gunmen. We're just a bunch of old cowhands and farmers. Call it anything you want. I call it murder."

"Yes!"

The word sliced through the room. Shane was up and his face was hard with the rock ridges running along his jaw. "Yes. It's murder. Trick it out as self-defense or with fancy words about an even break for a fair draw and it's still murder." He looked at father and the pain was deep in his eyes. But there was only contempt in his voice as he turned to the others.

"You five can crawl back in your burrows. You don't have to worry—yet. If the time comes, you can always sell and run. Fletcher won't bother with the likes of you now. He's going the limit and he knows the game. He picked Wright to make the play plain. That's done. Now he'll head straight for the one real man in this valley, the man who's held you here and will go on trying to hold you and keep for you what's yours as long as there's life in him. He's standing between you and Fletcher and Wilson this minute and you ought to be thankful that once in a while this country turns out a man like Joe Starrett."

And a man like Shane. . . . Were those words only in my mind or did I hear mother whisper them? She was looking at him and then at father and she was both frightened and proud at once. Father was fumbling with his pipe, packing it and making a fuss with it like it needed his whole attention.

The others stirred uneasily. They were reassured by what Shane said and yet shamed that they should be. And they did not like the way he said it.

"You seem to know a lot about that kind of dirty business," Ed Howells said, with maybe an edge of malice to his voice.

"I do."

Shane let the words lie there, plain and short and ugly. His face was stern and behind the hard front of his features was a sadness that fought to break through. But he stared levelly at Howells and it was the other man who dropped his eyes and turned away.

Father had his pipe going. "Maybe it's a lucky break for the rest of us," he said mildly, "that Shane here has been around a bit. He can call the cards for us plain. Ernie might still be alive, Johnson, if you had had the sense to tell us about Wilson right off. It's a good thing Ernie wasn't a family man." He turned to Shane. "How do you rate Fletcher now he's shown his hand?"

You could see that the chance to do something, even just to talk at the problem pressing us, eased the bitterness in Shane.

"He'll move in on Wright's place first thing tomorrow. He'll have a lot of men busy on this side of the river from now on, probably push some cattle around behind the homesteads, to keep the pressure plain on all of you. How quick he'll try you, Joe, depends on how he reads you. If he thinks you might crack, he'll wait and let knowing what happened to Wright work on you. If he really knows you, he'll not wait more than a day or two to make sure you've had time to think it over and then he'll grab the first chance to throw Wilson at you. He'll want it, like with Wright, in a public place where there'll be plenty of witnesses. If you don't give him a chance, he'll try to make one."

"Hm-m-m," father said soberly. "I was sure you'd give it to me straight and that rings right." He pulled on his pipe for a moment. "I reckon, boys, this will be a matter of waiting for the next few days. There's no immediate danger right off anyway. Grafton will take care of Ernie's body tonight. We can meet in town in the morning to fix him a funeral. After that, we'd better stay out of town and stick close to home as much as possible. I'd suggest you all study on this and drop in again tomorrow night. Maybe we can figure out something. I'd like to see how the town's taking it before I make up my mind on anything."

They were ready to leave it at that. They were ready to leave it to father. They were decent men and good neighbors. But not a one of them, were the decision his, would have stood up to Fletcher now. They would stay as long as father was there. With him gone, Fletcher would have things his way. That was how they felt as they muttered their goodnights and bunched out to scatter up and down the road.

Father stood in the doorway and watched them go. When he came back to his chair, he walked slowly and he seemed haggard and worn. "Somebody will have to go to Ernie's place tomorrow," he said, "and gather up his things. He's got relatives somewhere in Iowa."

"No." There was finality in Shane's tone. "You'll not go near the place. Fletcher might be counting on that. Grafton can do it."

"But Ernie was my friend," father said simply.

"Ernie's past friendship. Your debt is to the living."

Father looked at Shane and this brought him again into the immediate moment and cheered him. He nodded assent and turned to mother, who was hurrying to argue with him.

"Don't you see, Joe? If you can stay away from any place where you might meet Fletcher and—and that Wilson, things will work out. He can't keep a man like Wilson in this little valley forever."

She was talking rapidly and I knew why. She was not really trying to convince father as much as she was trying to convince herself. Father knew it, too.

"No, Marian. A man can't crawl into a hole somewhere and hide like a rabbit. Not if he has any pride."

"All right, then. But can't you keep quiet and not let him ride you and drive you into any fight?"

"That won't work either." Father was grim, but he was better and facing up to it. "A man can stand for a lot of pushing if he has to. 'Specially when he has his reasons." His glance shifted briefly to me. "But there are some things a man can't take. Not if he's to go on living with himself."

I was startled as Shane suddenly sucked in his breath with a long breaking intake. He was battling something within him, that old hidden desperation, and his eyes were dark and tormented against the paleness of his face. He seemed unable to look at us. He strode to the door and went out. We heard his footsteps fading toward the barn.

I was startled now at father. His breath, too, was coming in long, broken sweeps. He was up and pacing back and forth. When he swung on mother and his voice battered at her, almost fierce in its intensity, I realized that he knew about the change in Shane and that the knowing had been cankering in him all the past weeks.

"That's the one thing I can't stand, Marian. What we're doing to him. What happens to me doesn't matter too much. I talk big and I don't belittle myself. But my weight in any kind of a scale won't match his and I know it. If I understood him then as I do now, I'd never have got him to stay on here. But I didn't figure Fletcher would go this far. Shane won his fight before ever he came riding into this valley. It's been tough enough on him already. Should we let him lose just because of us? Fletcher can have his way. We'll sell out and move on."

I was not thinking. I was only feeling. For some strange reason I was feeling Shane's fingers in my hair, gently rocking my head. I could not help what I was saying, shouting across the room. "Father! Shane wouldn't run away! He wouldn't run away from anything!"

Father stopped pacing, his eyes narrowed in surprise. He stared at me without really seeing me. He was listening to mother.

"Bob's right, Joe. We can't let Shane down." It was queer, hearing her say the same thing to father she had said to Shane, the same thing with only the name different. "He'd never forgive us if we ran away from this. That's what we'd be doing. This isn't just a case of bucking Fletcher any more. It isn't just a case of keeping a piece of ground Fletcher wants for his range. We've got to be the kind of people Shane thinks we are. Bob's right. He wouldn't run away from anything like that. And that's the reason we can't."

"Lookahere, Marian, you don't think I want to do any running? No. You know me better than that. It'd go against everything in me. But what's my fool pride and this place and any plans we've had alongside of a man like that?"

"I know, Joe. But you don't see far enough." They were both talking earnestly, not breaking in, hearing each other out and sort of groping to put their meaning plain. "I can't really explain it, Joe. But I just know that we're bound up in something bigger than any one of us, and that running away is the one thing that would be worse than whatever might happen to us. There wouldn't be anything real ahead for us, any of us, maybe even for Bob, all the rest of our lives."

"Humph," said father. "Torrey could do it. And Johnson. All the rest of them. And it wouldn't bother them too much."

"Joe! Joe Starrett! Are you trying to make me mad? I'm not talking about them. I'm talking about us."

"Hm-m-m," said father softly, musing like to himself. "The salt would be gone. There just wouldn't be any flavor. There wouldn't be much meaning left."

"Oh, Joe! Joe! That's what I've been trying to say. And I know this will work out some way. I don't know how. But it will, if we face it and stand up to it and have faith in each other. It'll work out. Because it's got to."

"That's a woman's reason, Marian. But you're part right anyway. We'll play this game through. It'll need careful watching and close figuring. But maybe we can wait Fletcher out and make him overplay his hand. The town won't take much to this Wilson deal. Men like that fellow Weir have minds of their own."

Father was more cheerful now that he was beginning to get his thoughts straightened out. He and mother talked low in the kitchen for a long time after they sent me to bed, and I lay in my little room and saw through the window the stars wheeling distantly in the far outer darkness until I fell asleep at last.

12

THE MORNING SUN brightened our house and everything in the world outside. We had a good breakfast, father and Shane taking their time because they had routed out early to get the chores done and were waiting to go to town. They saddled up presently and rode off, and I moped in front of the house, not able to settle to any kind of playing.

After she bustled through the dishes, mother saw me standing and staring down the road and called me to the porch. She got our tattered old parchesi board and she kept me humping to beat her. She was a grand one for games like that. She would be as excited as a kid, squealing at the big numbers and doubles and counting proudly out loud as she moved her markers ahead.

When I had won three games running, she put the board away and brought out two fat apples and my favorite of the books she had from the time she taught school. Munching on her apple, she read to me and before I knew it the shadows were mighty short and she had to skip in to get dinner and father and Shane were riding up to the barn.

They came in while she was putting the food on the table. We sat down and it was almost like a holiday, not

just because it was not a work day, but because the grown
folks were talking lightly, were determined not to let this
Fletcher business spoil our good times. Father was pleased
at what had happened in town.

"Yes, sir," he was saying as we were finishing dinner.
"Ernie had a right good funeral. He would have appreci-
ated it. Grafton made a nice speech and, by Godfrey, I
believe he meant it. That fellow Weir had his clerk put
together a really fine coffin. Wouldn't take a cent for it.
And Sims over at the mine is knocking out a good stone.
He wouldn't take a cent either. I was surprised at the
crowd, too. Not a good word for Fletcher among them.
And there must have been thirty people there."

"Thirty-four," said Shane. "I counted 'em. They weren't
just paying their respects to Wright, Marian. That
wouldn't have brought in some of those I checked. They
were showing their opinion of a certain man named
Starrett, who made a pretty fair speech himself. This
husband of yours is becoming quite a respected citizen
in these parts. Soon as the town gets grown up and organized, he's likely to start going places. Give him time and
he'll be mayor."

Mother caught her breath with a little sob. "Give . . .
him . . . time," she said slowly. She looked at Shane and
there was panic in her eyes. The lightness was gone and
before anyone could say more, we heard the horses turning
into our yard.

I dashed to the window to peer out. It struck me strange
that Shane, usually so alert, was not there ahead of me.
Instead he pushed back his chair and spoke gently, still
sitting in it. "That will be Fletcher, Joe. He's heard how
the town is taking this and knows he has to move fast.
You take it easy. He's playing against time now, but he
won't push anything here."

Father nodded at Shane and went to the door. He had
taken off his gunbelt when he came in and now passed it
to lift the rifle from its nails on the wall. Holding it in
his right hand, barrel down, he opened the door and
stepped out on the porch, clear to the front edge. Shane

followed quietly and leaned in the doorway, relaxed and watchful. Mother was beside me at the window, staring out, crumpling her apron in her hand.

There were four of them, Fletcher and Wilson in the lead, two cowboys tagging. They had pulled up about twenty feet from the porch. This was the first time I had seen Fletcher for nearly a year. He was a tall man who must once have been a handsome figure in the fine clothes he always wore and with his arrogant air and his finely chiseled face set off by his short-cropped black beard and brilliant eyes. Now a heaviness was setting in about his features and a fatty softness was beginning to show in his body. His face had a shrewd cast and a kind of reckless determination was on him that I did not remember ever noticing before.

Stark Wilson, for all the dude look Frank Torrey had mentioned, seemed lean and fit. He was sitting idly in his saddle, but the pose did not fool you. He was wearing no coat and the two guns were swinging free. He was sure of himself, serene and deadly. The curl of his lip beneath his mustache was a combination of confidence in himself and contempt for us.

Fletcher was smiling and affable. He was certain he held the cards and was going to deal them as he wanted. "Sorry to bother you, Starrett, so soon after that unfortunate affair last night. I wish it could have been avoided. I really do. Shooting is so unnecessary in these things, if only people would show sense. But Wright never should have called Mr. Wilson here a liar. That was a mistake."

"It was," father said curtly. "But then Ernie always did believe in telling the truth." I could see Wilson stiffen and his lips tighten. Father did not look at him. "Speak your piece, Fletcher, and get off my land."

Fletcher was still smiling. "There's no call for us to quarrel, Starrett. What's done is done. Let's hope there's no need for anything like it to be done again. You've worked cattle on a big ranch and you can understand my position. I'll be wanting all the range I can get from now on. Even without that, I can't let a bunch of nesters keep coming in here and choke me off from my water rights."

"We've been over that before," father said. "You know where I stand. If you have more to say, speak up and be done with it."

"All right, Starrett. Here's my proposition. I like the way you do things. You've got some queer notions about the cattle business, but when you tackle a job, you take hold and do it thoroughly. You and that man of yours are a combination I could use. I want you on my side of the fence. I'm getting rid of Morgan and I want you to take over as foreman. From what I hear your man would make one hell of a driving trail boss. The spot's his. Since you've proved up on this place, I'll buy it from you. If you want to go on living here, that can be arranged. If you want to play around with that little herd of yours, that can be arranged too. But I want you working for me."

Father was surprised. He had not expected anything quite like this. He spoke softly to Shane behind him. He did not turn or look away from Fletcher, but his voice carried clearly.

"Can I call the turn for you, Shane?"

"Yes, Joe." Shane's voice was just as soft, but it, too, carried clearly and there was a little note of pride in it.

Father stood taller there on the edge of the porch. He stared straight at Fletcher. "And the others," he said slowly. "Johnson, Shipstead, and the rest. What about them?"

"They'll have to go."

Father did not hesitate. "No."

"I'll give you a thousand dollars for this place as it stands and that's my top offer."

"No."

The fury in Fletcher broke over his face and he started to turn in the saddle toward Wilson. He caught himself and forced again that shrewd smile. "There's no percentage in being hasty, Starrett. I'll boost the ante to twelve hundred. That's a lot better than what might happen if you stick to being stubborn. I'll not take an answer now. I'll give you till tonight to think it over. I'll be waiting at Grafton's to hear you talk sense."

He swung his horse and started away. The two cowboys turned to join him by the road. Wilson did not follow at once. He leaned forward in his saddle and drove a sneering look at father.

"Yes, Starrett. Think it over. You wouldn't like someone else to be enjoying this place of yours—and that woman there in the window."

He was lifting his reins with one hand to pull his horse around and suddenly he dropped them and froze to attention. It must have been what he saw in father's face. We could not see it, mother and I, because father's back was to us. But we could see his hand tightening on the rifle at his side.

"Don't, Joe!"

Shane was beside father. He slipped past, moving smooth and steady, down the steps and over to one side to come at Wilson on his right hand and stop not six feet from him. Wilson was puzzled and his right hand twitched and then was still as Shane stopped and as he saw that Shane carried no gun.

Shane looked up at him and Shane's voice flicked in a whiplash of contempt. "You talk like a man because of that flashy hardware you're wearing. Strip it away and you'd shrivel down to boy size."

The very daring of it held Wilson motionless for an instant and father's voice cut into it. "Shane! Stop it!"

The blackness faded from Wilson's face. He smiled grimly at Shane. "You do need someone to look after you." He whirled his horse and put it to a run to join Fletcher and the others in the road.

It was only then that I realized mother was gripping my shoulders so that they hurt. She dropped on a chair and held me to her. We could hear father and Shane on the porch.

"He'd have drilled you, Joe, before you could have brought the gun up and pumped in a shell."

"But you, you crazy fool!" Father was covering his feelings with a show of exasperation. "You'd have made him plug you just so I'd have a chance to get him."

Mother jumped up. She pushed me aside. She flared at them from the doorway. "And both of you would have acted like fools just because he said that about me. I'll have you two know that if it's got to be done, I can take being insulted just as much as you can."

Peering around her, I saw them gaping at her in astonishment. "But, Marian," father objected mildly, coming to her. "What better reason could a man have?"

"Yes," said Shane gently. "What better reason?" He was not looking just at mother. He was looking at the two of them.

13

I DO NOT KNOW how long they would have stood there on the porch in the warmth of that moment. I shattered it by asking what seemed to me a simple question until after I had asked it and the significance hit me.

"Father, what are you going to tell Fletcher tonight?"

There was no answer. There was no need for one. I guess I was growing up. I knew what he would tell Fletcher. I knew what he would say. I knew, too, that because he was father he would have to go to Grafton's and say it. And I understood why they could no longer bear to look at one another, and the breeze blowing in from the sun-washed fields was suddenly so chill and cheerless.

They did not look at each other. They did not say a word to each other. Yet somehow I realized that they were closer together in the stillness there on the porch than they had ever been. They knew themselves and each of them knew that the other grasped the situation whole. They knew that Fletcher had dealt himself a winning hand, had caught father in the one play that he could not avoid because he would not avoid it. They knew that talk is meaningless when a common knowledge is already there. The silence bound them as no words ever could.

Father sat on the top porch step. He took out his pipe and drew on it as the match flamed and fixed his eyes on the horizon, on the mountains far across the river. Shane took the chair I had used for the games with mother. He swung it to the house wall and bent into it in that familiar unconscious gesture and he, too, looked into the distance. Mother turned into the kitchen and went about clearing the table as if she was not really aware of what she was doing. I helped her with the dishes and the old joy of sharing with her in the work was gone and there was no sound in the kitchen except the drip of the water and the chink of dish on dish.

When we were done, she went to father. She sat beside him on the step, her hand on the wood between them, and his covered hers and the moments merged in the slow, dwindling procession of time.

Loneliness gripped me. I wandered through the house, finding nothing there to do, and out on the porch and past those three and to the barn. I searched around and found an old shovel handle and started to whittle me a play saber with my knife. I had been thinking of this for days. Now the idea held no interest. The wood curls dropped to the barn floor, and after a while I let the shovel handle drop among them. Everything that had happened before seemed far off, almost like another existence. All that mattered was the length of the shadows creeping across the yard as the sun drove down the afternoon sky.

I took a hoe and went into mother's garden where the ground was caked around the turnips, the only things left unharvested. But there was scant work in me. I kept at it for a couple of rows, then the hoe dropped and I let it lie. I went to the front of the house, and there they were sitting, just as before.

I sat on the step below father and mother, between them, and their legs on each side of me made it seem better. I felt father's hand on my head.

"This is kind of tough on you, Bob." He could talk to me because I was only a kid. He was really talking to himself.

"I can't see the full finish. But I can see this. Wilson

down and there'll be an end to it. Fletcher'll be done. The town will see to that. I can't beat Wilson on the draw. But there's strength enough in this clumsy body of mine to keep me on my feet till I get him, too." Mother stirred and was still, and his voice went on. "Things could be worse. It helps a man to know that if anything happens to him, his family will be in better hands than his own."

There was a sharp sound behind us on the porch. Shane had risen so swiftly that his chair had knocked against the wall. His hands were clenched tightly and his arms were quivering. His face was pale with the effort shaking him. He was desperate with an inner torment, his eyes tortured by thoughts that he could not escape, and the marks were obvious on him and he did not care. He strode to the steps, down past us and around the corner of the house.

Mother was up and after him, running headlong. She stopped abruptly at the house corner, clutching at the wood, panting and irresolute. Slowly she came back, her hands outstretched as if to keep from falling. She sank again on the step, close against father, and he gathered her to him with one great arm.

The silence spread and filled the whole valley and the shadows crept across the yard. They touched the road and began to merge in the deeper shading that meant the sun was dipping below the mountains far behind the house. Mother straightened, and as she stood up, father rose, too. He took hold of her two arms and held her in front of him. "I'm counting on you, Marian, to help him win again. You can do it, if anyone can." He smiled a strange little sad smile and he loomed up there above me the biggest man in all the world. "No supper for me now, Marian. A cup of your coffee is all I want." They passed through the doorway together.

Where was Shane? I hurried toward the barn. I was almost to it when I saw him out by the pasture. He was staring over it and the grazing steers at the great lonely mountains tipped with the gold of the sun now rushing down behind them. As I watched, he stretched his arms up, the fingers reaching to their utmost limits, grasping and grasping, it seemed, at the glory glowing in the sky.

He whirled and came straight back, striding with long steady steps, his head held high. There was some subtle, new, unchangeable certainty in him. He came close and I saw that his face was quiet and untroubled and that little lights danced in his eyes.

"Skip into the house, Bobby boy. Put on a smile. Everything is going to be all right." He was past me, without slowing, swinging into the barn.

But I could not go into the house. And I did not dare follow him, not after he had told me to go. A wild excitement was building up in me while I waited by the porch, watching the barn door.

The minutes ticked past and the twilight deepened and a patch of light sprang from the house as the lamp in the kitchen was lit. And still I waited. Then he was coming swiftly toward me and I stared and stared and broke and ran into the house with the blood pounding in my head.

"Father! Father! Shane's got his gun!"

He was close back of me. Father and mother barely had time to look up from the table before he was framed in the doorway. He was dressed as he was that first day when he rode into our lives, in that dark and worn magnificence from the black hat with its wide curling brim to the soft black boots. But what caught your eye was the single flash of white, the outer ivory plate on the grip of the gun, showing sharp and distinct against the dark material of the trousers. The tooled cartridge belt nestled around him, riding above the hip on the left, sweeping down on the right to hold the holster snug along the thigh, just as he had said, the gun handle about halfway between the wrist and elbow of his right arm hanging there relaxed and ready.

Belt and holster and gun . . . These were not things he was wearing or carrying. They were part of him, part of the man, of the full sum of the integrate force that was Shane. You could see now that for the first time this man who had been living with us, who was one of us, was complete, was himself in the final effect of his being.

Now that he was no longer in his crude work clothes, he seemed again slender, almost slight, as he did that first day. The change was more than that. What had been seeming iron was again steel. The slenderness was that of a tempered blade and a razor edge was there. Slim and dark in the doorway, he seemed somehow to fill the whole frame.

This was not our Shane. And yet it was. I remembered Ed Howells' saying that this was the most dangerous man he had ever seen. I remembered in the same rush that father had said he was the safest man we ever had in our house. I realized that both were right and that this, this at last, was Shane.

He was in the room now and he was speaking to them both in that bantering tone he used to have only for mother. "A fine pair of parents you are. Haven't even fed Bob yet. Stack him full of a good supper. Yourselves, too. I have a little business to tend to in town."

Father was looking fixedly at him. The sudden hope that had sprung in his face had as quickly gone. "No, Shane. It won't do. Even your thinking of it is the finest thing any man ever did for me. But I won't let you. It's my stand. Fletcher's making his play against me. There's no dodging. It's my business."

"There's where you're wrong, Joe," Shane said gently. "This is my business. My kind of business. I've had fun being a farmer. You've shown me new meaning in the word, and I'm proud that for a while maybe I qualified. But there are a few things a farmer can't handle."

The strain of the long afternoon was telling on father. He pushed up from the table. "Damn it, Shane, be sensible. Don't make it harder for me. You can't do this."

Shane stepped near, to the side of the table, facing father across a corner. "Easy does it, Joe. I'm making this my business."

"No. I won't let you. Suppose you do put Wilson out of the way. That won't finish anything. It'll only even the score and swing things back worse than ever. Think what it'll mean to you. And where will it leave me? I couldn't hold my head up around here any more. They'd say I ducked and they'd be right. You can't do it and that's that."

"No?" Shane's voice was even more gentle, but it had a quiet, inflexible quality that had never been there before.

"There's no man living can tell me what I can't do. Not even you, Joe. You forget there is still a way."

He was talking to hold father's attention. As he spoke the gun was in his hand and before father could move he swung it, swift and sharp, so the barrel lined flush along the side of father's head, back of the temple, above the ear. Strength was in the blow and it thudded dully on the bone and father folded over the table and as it tipped with his weight slid toward the floor. Shane's arm was under him before he hit and Shane pivoted father's loose body up and into his chair and righted the table while the coffee cups rattled on the floor boards. Father's head lolled back and Shane caught it and eased it and the big shoulders forward till they rested on the table, the face down and cradled in the limp arms.

Shane stood erect and looked across the table at mother. She had not moved since he appeared in the doorway, not even when father fell and the table teetered under her hands on its edge. She was watching Shane, her throat curving in a lovely proud line, her eyes wide with a sweet warmth shining in them.

Darkness had shut down over the valley as they looked at each other across the table and the only light now was from the lamp swinging ever so slightly above them, circling them with its steady glow. They were alone in a moment that was all their own. Yet, when they spoke, it was of father.

"I was afraid," Shane murmured, "that he would take it that way. He couldn't do otherwise and be Joe Starrett."

"I know."

"He'll rest easy and come out maybe a little groggy but all right. Tell him, Marian. Tell him no man need be ashamed of being beat by Shane."

The name sounded queer like that, the man speaking of himself. It was the closest he ever came to boasting. And then you understood that there was not the least hint of a boast. He was stating a fact, simple and elemental as the power that dwelled in him.

"I know," she said again. "I don't need to tell him. He knows, too." She was rising, earnest and intent. "But there

is something else I must know. We have battered down
words that might have been spoken between us and that
was as it should be. But I have a right to know now. I am
part of this, too. And what I do depends on what you tell
me now. Are you doing this just for me?"

Shane hesitated for a long, long moment. "No, Marian."
His gaze seemed to widen and encompass us all, mother
and the still figure of father and me huddled on a chair by
the window, and somehow the room and the house and
the whole place. Then he was looking only at mother and
she was all that he could see.

"No, Marian. Could I separate you in my mind and
afterwards be a man?"

He pulled his eyes from her and stared into the night
beyond the open door. His face hardened, his thoughts
leaping to what lay ahead in town. So quiet and easy you
were scarce aware that he was moving, he was gone into
the outer darkness.

14

NOTHING could have kept me there in the house that
night. My mind held nothing but the driving desire
to follow Shane. I waited, hardly daring to breathe, while
mother watched him go. I waited until she turned to father,
bending over him, then I slipped around the doorpost out
to the porch. I thought for a moment she had noticed me,
but I could not be sure and she did not call to me. I went
softly down the steps and into the freedom of the night.

Shane was nowhere in sight. I stayed in the darker
shadows, looking about, and at last I saw him emerging
once more from the barn. The moon was rising low over
the mountains, a clean, bright crescent. Its light was

enough for me to see him plainly in outline. He was carrying his saddle and a sudden pain stabbed through me as I saw that with it was his saddle-roll. He went toward the pasture gate, not slow, not fast, just firm and steady. There was a catlike certainty in his every movement, a silent, inevitable deadliness. I heard him, there by the gate, give his low whistle and the horse came out of the shadows at the far end of the pasture, its hooves making no noise in the deep grass, a dark and powerful shape etched in the moonlight drifting across the field straight to the man.

I knew what I would have to do. I crept along the corral fence, keeping tight to it, until I reached the road. As soon as I was around the corner of the corral with it and the barn between me and the pasture, I started to run as rapidly as I could toward town, my feet plumping softly in the thick dust of the road. I walked this every school day and it had never seemed long before. Now the distance stretched ahead, lengthening in my mind as if to mock me.

I could not let him see me. I kept looking back over my shoulder as I ran. When I saw him swinging into the road, I was well past Johnson's, almost past Shipstead's, striking into the last open stretch to the edge of town. I scurried to the side of the road and behind a clump of bullberry bushes. Panting to get my breath, I crouched there and waited for him to pass. The hoofbeats swelled in my ears, mingled with the pounding beat of my own blood. In my imagination he was galloping furiously and I was positive he was already rushing past me. But when I parted the bushes and pushed forward to peer out, he was moving at a moderate pace and was only almost abreast of me.

He was tall and terrible there in the road, looming up gigantic in the mystic half-light. He was the man I saw that first day, a stranger, dark and forbidding, forging his lone way out of an unknown past in the utter loneliness of his own immovable and instinctive defiance. He was the symbol of all the dim, formless imaginings of danger and terror in the untested realm of human potentialities beyond my understanding. The impact of the menace that marked him was like a physical blow.

I could not help it. I cried out and stumbled and fell. He was off his horse and over me before I could right myself, picking me up, his grasp strong and reassuring. I looked at him, tearful and afraid, and the fear faded from me. He was no stranger. That was some trick of the shadows. He was Shane. He was shaking me gently and smiling at me.

"Bobby boy, this is no time for you to be out. Skip along home and help your mother. I told you everything would be all right."

He let go of me and turned slowly, gazing out across the far sweep of the valley silvered in the moon's glow. "Look at it, Bob. Hold it in your mind like this. It's a lovely land, Bob. A good place to be a boy and grow straight inside as a man should."

My gaze followed his, and I saw our valley as though for the first time and the emotion in me was more than I could stand. I choked and reached out for him and he was not there.

He was rising into the saddle and the two shapes, the man and the horse, became one and moved down the road toward the yellow squares that were the patches of light from the windows of Grafton's building a quarter of a mile away. I wavered a moment, but the call was too strong. I started after him, running frantically in the middle of the road.

Whether he heard me or not, he kept right on. There were several men on the long porch of the building by the saloon doors. Red Marlin's hair made him easy to spot. They were scanning the road intently. As Shane hit the panel of light from the near big front window, the store window, they stiffened to attention. Red Marlin, a startled expression on his face, dived quickly through the doors.

Shane stopped, not by the rail but by the steps on the store side. When he dismounted, he did not slip the reins over the horse's head as the cowboys always did. He left them looped over the pommel of the saddle and the horse seemed to know what this meant. It stood motionless, close by the steps, head up, waiting, ready for whatever swift need.

Shane went along the porch and halted briefly, fronting the two men still there.

"Where's Fletcher?"

They looked at each other and at Shane. One of them started to speak. "He doesn't want—" Shane's voice stopped him. It slapped at them, low and with an edge that cut right into your mind. "Where's Fletcher?"

One of them jerked a hand toward the doors and then, as they moved to shift out of his way, his voice caught them.

"Get inside. Go clear to the bar before you turn."

They stared at him and stirred uneasily and swung together to push through the doors. As the doors came back, Shane grabbed them, one with each hand, and pulled them out and wide open and he disappeared between them.

Clumsy and tripping in my haste, I scrambled up the steps and into the store. Sam Grafton and Mr. Weir were the only persons there and they were both hurrying to the entrance to the saloon, so intent that they failed to notice me. They stopped in the opening. I crept behind them to my familiar perch on my box where I could see past them.

The big room was crowded. Almost everyone who could be seen regularly around town was there, everyone but our homestead neighbors. There were many others who were new to me. They were lined up elbow to elbow nearly the entire length of the bar. The tables were full and more men were lounging along the far wall. The big round poker table at the back between the stairway to the little balcony and the door to Grafton's office was littered with glasses and chips. It seemed strange, for all the men standing, that there should be an empty chair at the far curve of the table. Someone must have been in that chair, because chips were at the place and a half-smoked cigar, a wisp of smoke curling up from it, was by them on the table.

Red Marlin was leaning against the back wall, behind the chair. As I looked, he saw the smoke and appeared to start a little. With a careful show of casualness he slid into the chair and picked up the cigar.

A haze of thinning smoke was by the ceiling over them all, floating in involved streamers around the hanging lamps. This was Grafton's saloon in the flush of a banner evening's business. But something was wrong, was missing. The hum of activity, the whirr of voices, that should have risen from the scene, been part of it, was stilled in a hush more impressive than any noise could be. The attention of everyone in the room, like a single sense, was centered on that dark figure just inside the swinging doors, back to them and touching them.

This was the Shane of the adventures I had dreamed for him, cool and competent, facing that room full of men in the simple solitude of his own invincible completeness.

His eyes searched the room. They halted on a man sitting at a small table in the front corner with his hat on low over his forehead. With a thump of surprise I recognized it was Stark Wilson and he was studying Shane with a puzzled look on his face. Shane's eyes swept on, checking off each person. They stopped again on a figure over by the wall and the beginnings of a smile showed in them and he nodded almost imperceptibly. It was Chris, tall and lanky, his arm in a sling, and as he caught the nod he flushed a little and shifted his weight from one foot to the other. Then he straightened his shoulders and over his face came a slow smile, warm and friendly, the smile of a man who knows his own mind at last.

But Shane's eyes were already moving on. They narrowed as they rested on Red Marlin. Then they jumped to Will Atkey trying to make himself small behind the bar. "Where's Fletcher?"

Will fumbled with the cloth in his hands. "I—I don't know. He was here awhile ago." Frightened at the sound of his own voice in the stillness, Will dropped the cloth, started to stoop for it, and checked himself, putting his hands to the inside rim of the bar to hold himself steady.

Shane tilted his head slightly so his eyes could clear his hatbrim. He was scanning the balcony across the rear of the room. It was empty and the doors there were closed. He stepped forward, disregarding the men by the bar, and walked quietly past them the long length of the room.

He went through the doorway to Grafton's office and into the semi-darkness beyond.

And still the hush held. Then he was in the office doorway again and his eyes bored toward Red Marlin.

"Where's Fletcher?"

The silence was taut and unendurable. It had to break. The sound was that of Stark Wilson coming to his feet in the far front corner. His voice, lazy and insolent, floated down the room.

"Where's Starrett?"

While the words yet seemed to hang in the air, Shane was moving toward the front of the room. But Wilson was moving, too. He was crossing toward the swinging doors and he took his stand just to the left of them, a few feet out from the wall. The position gave him command of the wide aisle running back between the bar and the tables and Shane coming forward in it.

Shane stopped about three quarters of the way forward, about five yards from Wilson. He cocked his head for one quick sidewise glance again at the balcony and then he was looking only at Wilson. He did not like the setup. Wilson had the front wall and he was left in the open of the room. He understood the fact, assessed it, accepted it.

They faced each other in the aisle and the men along the bar jostled one another in their hurry to get to the opposite side of the room. A reckless arrogance was on Wilson, certain of himself and his control of the situation. He was not one to miss the significance of the slim deadliness that was Shane. But even now, I think, he did not believe that anyone in our valley would deliberately stand up to him.

"Where's Starrett?" he said once more, still mocking Shane but making it this time a real question.

The words went past Shane as if they had not been spoken. "I had a few things to say to Fletcher," he said gently. "That can wait. You're a pushing man, Wilson, so I reckon I had better accommodate you."

Wilson's face sobered and his eyes glinted coldly. "I've no quarrel with you," he said flatly, "even if you are Starrett's man. Walk out of here without any fuss and I'll let you go. It's Starrett I want."

"What you want, Wilson, and what you'll get are two different things. Your killing days are done."

Wilson had it now. You could see him grasp the meaning. This quiet man was pushing him just as he had pushed Ernie Wright. As he measured Shane, it was not to his liking. Something that was not fear but a kind of wondering and baffled reluctance showed in his face. And then there was no escape, for that gentle voice was pegging him to the immediate and implacable moment.

"I'm waiting, Wilson. Do I have to crowd you into slapping leather?"

Time stopped and there was nothing in all the world but two men looking into eternity in each other's eyes. And the room rocked in the sudden blur of action indistinct in its incredible swiftness and the roar of their guns was a single sustained blast. And Shane stood, solid on his feet as a rooted oak, and Wilson swayed, his right arm hanging useless, blood beginning to show in a small stream from under the sleeve over the hand, the gun slipping from the numbing fingers.

He backed against the wall, a bitter disbelief twisting his features. His left arm hooked and the second gun was showing and Shane's bullet smashed into his chest and his knees buckled, sliding him slowly down the wall till the lifeless weight of the body toppled it sideways to the floor.

Shane gazed across the space between and he seemed to have forgotten all else as he let his gun ease into the holster. "I gave him his chance," he murmured out of the depths of a great sadness. But the words had no meaning for me, because I noticed on the dark brown of his shirt, low and just above the belt to one side of the buckle, the darker spot gradually widening. Then others noticed, too, and there was a stir in the air and the room was coming to life.

Voices were starting, but no one focused on them. They were snapped short by the roar of a shot from the rear of the room. A wind seemed to whip Shane's shirt at the shoulder and the glass of the front window beyond shattered near the bottom.

Then I saw it.

It was mine alone. The others were turning to stare at
the back of the room. My eyes were fixed on Shane and I
saw it. I saw the whole man move, all of him, in the single
flashing instant. I saw the head lead and the body swing
and the driving power of the legs beneath. I saw the arm
leap and the hand take the gun in the lightning sweep. I
saw the barrel line up like—like a finger pointing—and
the flame spurt even as the man himself was still in motion.

And there on the balcony Fletcher, impaled in the act
of aiming for a second shot, rocked on his heels and fell
back into the open doorway behind him. He clawed at
the jambs and pulled himself forward. He staggered to the
rail and tried to raise the gun. But the strength was drain-
ing out of him and he collapsed over the rail, jarring it
loose and falling with it.

Across the stunned and barren silence of the room
Shane's voice seemed to come from a great distance. "I
expect that finishes it," he said. Unconsciously, without
looking down, he broke out the cylinder of his gun and
reloaded it. The stain on his shirt was bigger now, spreading fanlike above the belt, but he did not appear to know
or care. Only his movements were slow, retarded by an
unutterable weariness. The hands were sure and steady,
but they moved slowly and the gun dropped into the
holster of its own weight.

He backed with dragging steps toward the swinging
doors until his shoulders touched them. The light in his
eyes was unsteady like the flickering of a candle guttering
toward darkness. And then, as he stood there, a strange
thing happened.

How could one describe it, the change that came over
him? Out of the mysterious resources of his will the vitality came. It came creeping, a tide of strength that crept
through him and fought and shook off the weakness. It
shone in his eyes and they were alive again and alert. It
welled up in him, sending that familiar power surging
through him again until it was singing again in every
vibrant line of him.

He faced that room full of men and read them all with

the one sweeping glance and spoke to them in that gentle voice with that quiet, inflexible quality.

"I'll be riding on now. And there's not a one of you that will follow."

He turned his back on them in the indifference of absolute knowledge they would do as he said. Straight and superb, he was silhouetted against the doors and the patch of night above them. The next moment they were closing with a soft swish of sound.

The room was crowded with action now. Men were clustering around the bodies of Wilson and Fletcher, pressing to the bar, talking excitedly. Not a one of them, though, approached too close to the doors. There was a cleared space by the doorway as if someone had drawn a line marking it off.

I did not care what they were doing or what they were saying. I had to get to Shane. I had to get to him in time. I had to know, and he was the only one who could ever tell me.

I dashed out the store door and I was in time. He was on his horse, already starting away from the steps.

"Shane," I whispered desperately, loud as I dared without the men inside hearing me. "Oh, Shane!"

He heard me and reined around and I hurried to him, standing by a stirrup and looking up.

"Bobby! Bobby boy! What are you doing here?"

"I've been here all along," I blurted out. "You've got to tell me. Was that Wilson—"

He knew what was troubling me. He always knew. "Wilson," he said, "was mighty fast. As fast as I've ever seen."

"I don't care," I said, the tears starting. "I don't care if he was the fastest that ever was. He'd never have been able to shoot you, would he? You'd have got him straight, wouldn't you—if you had been in practice?"

He hesitated a moment. He gazed down at me and into me and he knew. He knew what goes on in a boy's mind and what can help him stay clean inside through the muddled, dirtied years of growing up.

"Sure. Sure, Bob. He'd never even have cleared the holster."

He started to bend down toward me, his hand reaching for my head. But the pain struck him like a whiplash and the hand jumped to his shirt front by the belt, pressing hard, and he reeled a little in the saddle.

The ache in me was more than I could bear. I stared dumbly at him, and because I was just a boy and helpless I turned away and hid my face against the firm, warm flank of the horse.

"Bob."

"Yes, Shane."

"A man is what he is, Bob, and there's no breaking the mold. I tried that and I've lost. But I reckon it was in the cards from the moment I saw a freckled kid on a rail up the road there and a real man behind him, the kind that could back him for the chance another kid never had."

"But—but, Shane, you—"

"There's no going back from a killing, Bob. Right or wrong, the brand sticks and there's no going back. It's up to you now. Go home to your mother and father. Grow strong and straight and take care of them. Both of them."

"Yes, Shane."

"There's only one thing more I can do for them now."

I felt the horse move away from me. Shane was looking down the road and on to the open plain and the horse was obeying the silent command of the reins. He was riding away and I knew that no word or thought could hold him. The big horse, patient and powerful, was already settling into the steady pace that had brought him into our valley, and the two, the man and the horse, were a single dark shape in the road as they passed beyond the reach of the light from the windows.

I strained my eyes after him, and then in the moonlight I could make out the inalienable outline of his figure receding into the distance. Lost in my loneliness, I watched him go, out of town, far down the road where it curved out to the level country beyond the valley. There were men on the porch behind me, but I was aware only of that dark shape growing small and indistinct along the far reach of the road. A cloud passed over the moon and he merged into the general shadow and I could not see him and the cloud passed on and the road was a plain thin ribbon to the horizon and he was gone.

I stumbled back to fall on the steps, my head in my arms to hide the tears. The voices of the men around me were meaningless noises in a bleak and empty world. It was Mr. Weir who took me home.

15

FATHER AND MOTHER were in the kitchen, almost as I had left them. Mother had hitched her chair close to father's. He was sitting up, his face tired and haggard, the ugly red mark standing out plain along the side of his head. They did not come to meet us. They sat still and watched us move into the doorway.

They did not even scold me. Mother reached and pulled me to her and let me crawl into her lap as I had not done for three years or more. Father just stared at Mr. Weir. He could not trust himself to speak first.

"Your troubles are over, Starrett."

Father nodded. "You've come to tell me," he said wearily, "that he killed Wilson before they got him. I know. He was Shane."

"Wilson," said Mr. Weir. "And Fletcher."

Father started. "Fletcher, too? By Godfrey, yes. He would do it right." Then father sighed and ran a finger along the bruise on his head. "He let me know this was one thing he wanted to handle by himself. I can tell you, Weir, waiting here is the hardest job I ever had."

Mr. Weir looked at the bruise. "I thought so. Listen,

Starrett. There's not a man in town doesn't know you didn't stay here of your own will. And there's damn few that aren't glad it was Shane came into the saloon tonight."

The words broke from me. "You should have seen him, father. He was—he was—" I could not find it at first. "He was—beautiful, father. And Wilson wouldn't even have hit him if he'd been in practice. He told me so."

"He told you!" The table was banging over as father drove to his feet. He grabbed Mr. Weir by the coat front. "My God, man! Why didn't you tell me? He's alive?"

"Yes," said Mr. Weir. "He's alive all right. Wilson got to him. But no bullet can kill that man." A puzzled, far-away sort of look flitted across Mr. Weir's face. "Sometimes I wonder whether anything ever could."

Father was shaking him. "Where is he?"

"He's gone," said Mr. Weir. "He's gone, alone and unfollowed as he wanted it. Out of the valley and no one knows where."

Father's hands dropped. He slumped again into his chair. He picked up his pipe and it broke in his fingers. He let the pieces fall and stared at them on the floor. He was still staring at them when new footsteps sounded on the porch and a man pushed into our kitchen.

It was Chris. His right arm was tight in the sling, his eyes unnaturally bright and the color high in his face. In his left hand he was carrying a bottle, a bottle of red cherry soda pop. He came straight in and righted the table with the hand holding the bottle. He smacked the bottle on the top boards and seemed startled at the noise he made. He was embarrassed and he was having trouble with his voice. But he spoke up firmly.

"I brought that for Bob. I'm a damned poor substitute, Starrett. But as soon as this arm's healed, I'm asking you to let me work for you."

Father's face twisted and his lips moved, but no words came. Mother was the one who said it. "Shane would like that, Chris."

And still father said nothing. What Chris and Mr. Weir saw as they looked at him must have shown them that nothing they could do or say would help at all. They turned and went out together, walking with long, quick steps.

Mother and I sat there watching father. There was nothing we could do either. This was something he had to wrestle alone. He was so still that he seemed even to have stopped breathing. Then a sudden restlessness hit him and he was up and pacing aimlessly about. He glared at the walls as if they stifled him and strode out the door into the yard. We heard his steps around the house and heading into the fields and then we could hear nothing.

I do not know how long we sat there. I know that the wick in the lamp burned low and sputtered awhile and went out and the darkness was a relief and a comfort. At last mother rose, still holding me, the big boy bulk of me, in her arms. I was surprised at the strength in her. She was holding me tightly to her and she carried me into my little room and helped me undress in the dim shadows of the moonlight through the window. She tucked me in and sat on the edge of the bed, and then, only then, she whispered to me: "Now, Bob. Tell me everything. Just as you saw it happen."

I told her, and when I was done, all she said in a soft little murmur was "Thank you." She looked out the window and murmured the words again and they were not for me and she was still looking out over the land to the great gray mountains when finally I fell asleep.

She must have been there the whole night through, for when I woke with a start, the first streaks of dawn were showing through the window and the bed was warm where she had been. The movement of her leaving must have wakened me. I crept out of bed and peeked into the kitchen. She was standing in the open outside doorway.

I fumbled into my clothes and tiptoed through the kitchen to her. She took my hand and I clung to hers and it was right that we should be together and that together we should go find father.

We found him out by the corral, by the far end where Shane had added to it. The sun was beginning to rise through the cleft in the mountains across the river, not the brilliant glory of midday but the fresh and renewed reddish radiance of early morning. Father's arms were folded on the top rail, his head bowed on them. When he turned to face us, he leaned back against the rail as if he needed the support. His eyes were rimmed and a little wild.

"Marian, I'm sick of the sight of this valley and all that's in it. If I tried to stay here now, my heart wouldn't be in it any more. I know it's hard on you and the boy, but we'll have to pull up stakes and move on. Montana, maybe. I've heard there's good land for the claiming up that way."

Mother heard him through. She had let go my hand and stood erect, so angry that her eyes snapped and her chin quivered. But she heard him through.

"Joe! Joe Starrett!" Her voice fairly crackled and was rich with emotion that was more than anger. "So you'd run out on Shane just when he's really here to stay?"

"But, Marian. You don't understand. He's gone."

"He's not gone. He's here, in this place, in this place he gave us. He's all around us and in us, and he always will be."

She ran to the tall corner post, to the one Shane had set. She beat at it with her hands. "Here, Joe. Quick. Take hold. Pull it down."

Father stared at her in amazement. But he did as she said. No one could have denied her in that moment. He took hold of the post and pulled at it. He shook his head and braced his feet and strained at it with all his strength. The big muscles of his shoulders and back knotted and bulged till I thought this shirt, too, would shred. Creakings ran along the rails and the post moved ever so slightly and the ground at the base showed little cracks fanning out. But the rails held and the post stood.

Father turned from it, beads of sweat breaking on his face, a light creeping up his drawn cheeks.

"See, Joe. See what I mean. We have roots here now that we can never tear loose."

And the morning was in father's face, shining in his eyes, giving him new color and hope and understanding.

16

I GUESS that is all there is to tell. The folks in town and the kids at school liked to talk about Shane, to spin tales and speculate about him. I never did. Those nights at Grafton's became legends in the valley and countless details were added as they grew and spread just as the town, too, grew and spread up the river banks. But I never bothered, no matter how strange the tales became in the constant retelling. He belonged to me, to father and mother and me, and nothing could ever spoil that.

For mother was right. He was there. He was there in our place and in us. Whenever I needed him, he was there. I could close my eyes and he would be with me and I would see him plain and hear again that gentle voice.

I would think of him in each of the moments that revealed him to me. I would think of him most vividly in that single flashing instant when he whirled to shoot Fletcher on the balcony at Grafton's saloon. I would see again the power and grace of a coordinate force beautiful beyond comprehension. I would see the man and the weapon wedded in the one indivisible deadliness. I would see the man and the tool, a good man and a good tool, doing what had to be done.

And always my mind would go back at the last to that moment when I saw him from the bushes by the roadside just on the edge of town. I would see him there in the road, tall and terrible in the moonlight, going down to kill or be killed, and stopping to help a stumbling boy and to look out over the land, the lovely land, where that boy had a chance to live out his boyhood and grow straight inside as a man should.

And when I would hear the men in town talking among themselves and trying to pin him down to a definite past, I would smile quietly to myself. For a time they inclined to the notion, spurred by the talk of a passing stranger, that he was a certain Shannon who was famous as a gunman and gambler way down in Arkansas and Texas and dropped from sight without anyone knowing why or where. When that notion dwindled, others followed, pieced together in turn from scraps of information gleaned from stray travelers. But when they talked like that, I simply smiled because I knew he could have been none of these.

He was the man who rode into our little valley out of the heart of the great glowing West and when his work was done rode back whence he had come and he was Shane.

Which of these Pathfinders have you missed?

- [ ] **SP114** (75¢)   **A PLANET CALLED EARTH**, George Gamow. A life history of our world from its birth to its expected death.

- [ ] **EP73** (45¢)   **THE SEA OF GRASS**, Conrad Richter. The unforgettable novel of the great days of early Texas.

- [ ] **SP97** (75¢)   **THE GOOD YEARS**, Walter Lord. The fabulous story of America's golden era of 1900-1914.

- [ ] **HP61** (60¢)   **DANCE TO THE PIPER**, Agnes de Mille. The fascinating life story of one of America's greatest dancers.

- [ ] **HP92** (60¢)   **IDYLLS OF THE KING**, Alfred Lord Tennyson. A great poet's magnificent retelling of the King Arthur legend.

- [ ] **FP91** (50¢)   **THE SCARLET LETTER**, Nathaniel Hawthorne. The great American novel of guilt and redemption.

- [ ] **FP69** (50¢)   **APRIL MORNING**, Howard Fast. The making of a man, a nation and a way of life during the Battle of Lexington.

- [ ] **FP106** (50¢)   **THE INCREDIBLE JOURNEY**, Sheila Burnford. The inspiring story of a bull terrier, a Siamese cat, and a Labrador retriever's incredible journey across the trackless wastes of the Canadian wilds.

- [ ] **FP75** (50¢)   **TEN TOP STORIES**, David Sohn, ed. A unique collection of stories about young adults.

- [ ] **FP53** (50¢)   **SEVENTEEN**, Booth Tarkington. The pathos and humor of a boy's first love.

AVAILABLE AT NEWSSTANDS EVERYWHERE

UNFORGETTABLE READING

TWO EXCITING NOVELS BY HENRY FELSEN

HOT ROD The thrill-packed story of a daring young driver and his souped-up jalopy which could hit a sweet 120 miles an hour. 50c ☐

CRASH CLUB When Dave Galt moved into town he threatened Mike's title as "top man." Mike's answer to Galt's bid for power was a new kind of hot rod club—crash club. 45c ☐

UNFORGETTABLE READING

THE INCREDIBLE JOURNEY by SHEILA BURNFORD. The heart warming story of a Labrador retriever, a bull terrier, and a Siamese cat and their epic journey across the Canadian wilderness in the dead of winter to return to the family they love. 50c ☐

APRIL MORNING by HOWARD FAST. The exciting story of a young boy living in revolutionary America who suddenly becomes a man during the battle of Lexington. 50c ☐